"I thought you said you'd follow me any-where."

He was grinning from ear to ear as he put his head out the window.

Angeline was terrified and shaking so hard she didn't think she'd be able to move. The voices in the hall grew louder and one of them clearly became recognizable as Douglas. Without second thoughts, she was out the window and standing beside Gavin on the ledge.

Trembling with her back against the cold brick wall, Angeline thought she would die. She felt Gavin's warm hand on her arm and prayed God would rescue them from their perch. She heard Gavin lower the window and scoot closer to her.

"It's going to be alright, Angel. You'll see."

"Oh, Gavin," she said and her voice was full of emotion. "What if I faint out here?"

"You won't," he said confidently. "Open your eyes and look at me, Angel." She did without considering the consequences. "God's with us. He's been with us from the start, but I think maybe you're just learning that. I love you and I'm not about to let anything happen to you. Especially not now that you've agreed to be my wife. You will be my wife, won't you, Angel?"

Angeline looked deep into Gavin's eyes. There was barely enough light from the window to reflect the love he held for her there. "If we live through this," she whispered, "I'll most gratefully marry you."

Gavin chuckled and kissed her forehead. "Good, now don't look down and keep quiet. Someday you can tell our children how I proposed on a ledge three stories above Denver."

Tracie J. Peterson is a popular inspirational writer and a regular columnist for a Christian newspaper in Topeka, Kansas. Tracie has also written eight successful **Heartsong Presents** titles under the name of Janelle Jamison.

HEARTSONG PRESENTS

Books by Janelle Jamison

HP19—A Place to Belong
HP40—Perfect Love
HP47—Tender Journeys
HP56—A Light in the Window
HP63—The Willing Heart
HP71—Destiny's Road
HP88—Beyond Today
HP93—Iditarod Dream

Books by Tracie J. Peterson

HP102—If Given a Choice
HP111—A Kingdom Divided
HP127—Forever Yours

Don't miss out on any of our super romances. Write to us at the following address for information on our newest releases and club information.

Heartsong Presents Readers' Service
P.O. Box 719
Uhrichsville, OH 44683

Angel's Cause

Tracie J. Peterson

Heartsong Presents

Dedicated to:

Ramona Kelly—*with a glad and grateful heart that God has blessed me with our continuing friendship. I love you!*

Clara Norris—*God crossed our paths a long time ago and I've been the better for it. I love you!*

A note from the Author:
I love to hear from my readers! You may correspond with me by writing:

> **Tracie J. Peterson**
> **Author Relations**
> **P.O. Box 719**
> **Uhrichsville, OH 44683**

ISBN 1-55748-764-2

ANGEL'S CAUSE

Cover illustration by Kathy Arbuckle.

PRINTED IN THE U.S.A.

one

Angeline Monroe peeked out from behind her frilly parasol and giggled. At eighteen, she was clearly one of the most beautiful, if not the most beautiful girl in all of north-central New Mexico. The proof of this was the circle of young men that followed her around like a pack of lost pups, each one trying to out do the other for her attention. Each one completely captivated with the charming wiles of the shapely young woman.

Her parents struggled to take their daughter's popularity in stride. It wasn't that they didn't want Angeline to court and marry, but the attention that seemed to follow their youngest child was often a worrisome thing.

"You don't suppose we could just put her in a convent?" Daniel Monroe asked his wife in mock seriousness.

Lillie Monroe was an older version of her daughter Angeline. Something in the way her daughter moved among the circle of suitors reminded her of herself. With a laugh she turned to her husband. "You're too old fashioned, Doctor."

Daniel ran a hand through his hair as had been his habit for over fifty years. "She seems too young."

"She is eighteen."

Daniel winced. Where had the years gone?

Angeline was oblivious to her parent's concern. She loved being courted, even if it was by the entire bachelor population of Bandelero, New Mexico. Even if they did it all at one time.

Church picnics were the best, Angeline decided, while demurely evaluating her companions. Everyone got to wear pretty clothes and look nice, because you'd just come from services. Then you'd spread out blankets down by the river and everyone would eat and talk and laugh. Yes, church picnics were the very best way to get to know each other.

She put a hand up to brush back a tiny wisp of invisible hair. It made her appear quite innocent and positively feminine, she knew. She knew, of course, because she'd practiced doing this very thing in front of her bedroom mirror.

Angeline glanced coyly around her to make certain her audience was still captive to her cause. Causes were very important to Angeline. She'd joined one after the other and always threw herself into the working needs of each. She supposed the very first cause she'd ever joined was that of Christianity. To Angeline, going to church and participating in the various activities and committees was a prime cause, indeed. And, in this situation, the cause did her a great deal of good. Her parents often felt that she needed to take the matter of spirituality more seriously, but Angeline noted that she lived by the Good Book and was wholly devoted to the various missionary projects. It was hard to understand why her parents would even once question her devotion to spiritual matters.

Leaving the distastefulness of such thoughts behind, Angeline passed a glance over each young man, receiving in return looks that ran the range from shyly embarrassed to boldly inviting. *Men!* she thought to herself, nearly laughing out loud. How simple minded they were.

Suddenly, as a mother might be aware of one child's absence from her brood, Angeline realized that she did not command the attention of every bachelor at the picnic. One very stubborn man stood off under a tree and looked to Angeline to be quite bored with the entire day.

Gavin Lucas, oldest son of Maggie and Garrett Lucas, refused to join his four brothers in the pursuit of Angeline Monroe. He watched, however. Very discretely so as not to draw attention to himself. He saw his brothers Joseph, Jordy, and twins Dolan and Don while they seemed to dance on a puppet string that Angeline controlled. No, he wasn't about to play that game.

And, it was because he wouldn't play the game that Angeline even noticed him. She'd always liked the Lucas boys. Maybe it was because her parents and theirs were life long friends. Maybe it was because for so many years there had hardly been anyone else around. Then one day the railroad came to Bandelero and the town began to boom, bringing new people, new businesses and a whole new lifestyle. Overnight it seemed, the town had grown from twenty or thirty to five hundred and then a thousand. It was a little smaller now because interest seemed to pull people south to Santa Fe and Albuquerque or north to Denver and Colorado Springs. But no matter. Angeline knew how to make the most of what she had and there was always a cause to be found to entertain herself with.

"Why won't you take a walk with me down by the river?" Jordy Lucas was saying. A full year younger than herself, Angeline never seriously considered Jordy when thinking of husband material. And if she couldn't consider him for that, why waste her time walking by the river?

"I'm having too much fun," she said, beaming a broad smile upon all of them. "I want to stay right here and enjoy the day."

It seemed as though everyone started talking at once then,

but Angeline's eyes were once again drawn to Gavin. He hadn't moved in the last half hour and Angeline couldn't help but wonder what he was so seriously considering.

❧

Gavin smiled to himself, knowing that Angeline, or Angel as he had called her since she was a child, was disturbed by his aloofness. Up until the last year or so, he'd played her game just like the others. Now, Gavin was through playing. He'd made up his mind about Angel over two years ago and now he was just biding his time. Angeline Monroe was the woman he intended to marry. She just didn't know it yet. Shoving his hands deep into his trouser pockets, Gavin pretended to study the leaves overhead.

"What are you doing here all by yourself?" Daughtry Dawson, Gavin's married sister, asked thrusting a small boy into his arms. "You might as well watch over Kent for me while I help get the food on the table."

Gavin's serious expression changed into surprise and then honest pleasure. "How ya doin', partner?" Kent, barely a year old, looked up at his uncle and squealed.

"I guess that means good," Daughtry replied, tucking a stray strand of copper hair back into place. "Do you mind keeping an eye on him for me?"

"Not at all," Gavin said, burying his face against the baby's stomach and growling. Kent began to chortle in his baby way. Gavin then held him high into the air, bouncing him up and down.

"Thanks, Gavin," Daughtry said almost apologetically and slipped away while Kent was preoccupied.

Gavin looked past the baby nonchalantly. *Good,* he thought. *Now I really have Angel's attention.* He knew Angeline would come to him on the pretense of playing with Kent, but in truth it would be Gavin she was seeking out. That and the reason for why he was no longer playing her game. Turning his back to Angel and her crowd of suitors, Gavin began to count.

"One!" he said and lifted Kent high into the air. "Two!" he counted and swung the boy low to the ground. Kent giggled and clapped his hands, when he wasn't gripping Gavin's arm.

"Three!" Gavin had just brought Kent up even with his head, when Angeline's voice sounded from behind him.

"Hello, Gavin," she said, seeming to purr the words. "I saw that you were playing with Kent and I just had to come see him."

Gavin stopped swinging Kent and turned to face Angeline. Meeting her eyes, a color somewhere between lavender and blue, he hid the effect she always had on him. "Hi, Angel."

Angeline had his attention now, so she moved on to capture Kent's. No man, no matter the age, was safe from her charms. Holding her arms up to Kent, he immediately went to her from Gavin.

"You are just the sweetest thing." Angeline's voice rang out like a song. Kent reached for a handful of her long blond curls and laughingly pulled them to his mouth.

"Better not, partner," Gavin said, using the excuse to touch Angel's hair. He gently removed the spun gold strands from Kent's grubby hands and let the hair curl around his own fingers for just a moment. It was soft and fine like silk and Gavin silently wished he could bury his hands in it as his nephew had.

Angeline smiled smugly at the exchange, knowing that Gavin was now hers to command. "You're such a little darlin'," Angeline drawled softly, kissing Kent on the forehead. Then without missing a beat, she looked up at Gavin and smiled. "How come you're here by yourself? I missed you."

Gavin let a slow lop-sided grin overtake his normally serious expression. "I'm surprised you even noticed me. What happened to your choir?"

"My what?" Angeline questioned, feigning serious confusion.

"Your choir. I figured what with the moaning and groaning of that group, they must be warming up for a good song."

Angeline laughed in spite of the fact that she'd planned not to respond to anything Gavin said. "Jealous?" she finally asked.

"Nope," Gavin stated, quite serious, and took Kent from Angeline's arms. "Never did like to sing." With that he walked off to leave Angeline to stare after him. He wanted to laugh out loud at the stunned expression on her face, but he held it back. She'd come around in time.

≈

Two days later, Angeline was still stinging from Gavin's rejection. She'd played the scene over in her mind and saw no reason for his rudeness. She evaluated scenes from weeks, months, and even years gone by and wondered silently when Gavin had lost interest in her. Did it matter? she couldn't help but ask herself. Then, deciding that it shouldn't, Angeline went to work to find a new cause to occupied herself with.

At supper, Angeline had decided what she would request. She waited for just the exact moment when her mother put desert and a fresh pot of coffee on the table. If her luck held, Angeline thought, no one would call for her father to come play doctor. If her luck held, she just might get her own way.

"Mother, Father," Angeline began and both of her parents looked up warily. "I have something to ask you."

Dan looked at Lillie as Lillie was looking to Dan. They were searching each other for a clue as to what Angeline had planned. When both shrugged, they turned their attention to Angeline and collectively held their breath.

"I want to travel." Angeline was never one to beat around an issue. She was well known for coming right out with what she wanted. "I know I can't go abroad what with that dreadful war in Europe." She made the affair sound as if it were a party out of control, rather than a life and death battle of political issues.

Angeline smiled sweetly at both of her parents before continuing. "I know too, that you miss John and James since they've gone off to join the army." She waited to see if they would say anything. She almost felt sorry for being the cause of the stunned expression on their faces. "Anyway, I would very much like to travel and see some of our other states. California, for instance, and New York. I've read so much about both places as well as Chicago and Kansas City. I really do want to see these cities."

Dan was the first to speak. "Angeline, you can't very well go off by yourself and your mother and I can't just pick up and leave. We have obligations and duties here."

"Your father is right," Lillie said, but her memory reminded her that she too had enjoyed traveling as a young lady. "We can't very well take you on any extended trips." Lillie glanced at Daniel, hoping he might soften the blow somehow. Neither one was very good at telling Angeline, "no."

Angeline grew very serious. Her eyes seemed to plead from the softness of her heart-shaped face. "I feel so pressured here," she said softly. "Everyone expects me to choose a man and get married and I'm just not ready for that yet." It was the very thing to get Lillie and Daniel's mind, in line with Angeline's desires.

"Nobody says you have to get married," Daniel stated

firmly. "I certainly haven't been pushing you to find a husband."

"Nor I," Lillie added.

"I know," Angeline said in her manipulative way. "But nevertheless, it is expected. Why just the other day I heard, well, it wasn't very nice and I shan't repeat it in full." Angeline paused as if it pained her greatly to continue.

"What did you hear?" Lillie and Daniel asked in unison.

"Well, there was some talk about how dreadfully old Daughtry Lucas was when she got married. She was nearly twenty-four, you know."

Lillie and Daniel smiled at each other. Twenty-four must seem quite ancient to their daughter.

"Anyway, people just seem to naturally think I should be looking to marry right away. Of course, there are other obligations to consider, since I'm the last one at home. You know how people are these days. Especially in regards to obligations."

Lillie's eyes narrowed just a bit. "What do you mean?"

Angeline smiled. "I suppose people just worry that I'll stay here and take care of you and Papa. Sometimes it's just expected of unmarried women."

"What is?" Daniel asked, completely baffled by Angeline's line of discussion.

"That I remain unmarried in order to care for you and Mother, in your aging years."

"What!?" Daniel and Lillie exclaimed at once.

"Not that I would mind all that much, but I would like to see at least a bit of the country before I did that."

Daniel started laughing, which in turn made Lillie giggle. Angeline pretended to be confused. But even so, it was hard to know what her parents were thinking and some of her confusion was genuine.

"Did I say something wrong?" she questioned respectfully.

"No, sweetheart," Daniel replied. "It's just that your mother and I are far from ready to be cared for. I think we can surely find some way to stretch your mind a bit, if not your legs. What do you say you let us consider the matter of travel? Maybe we could find a suitable traveling companion for you or maybe I could spare your mother for a week or so."

"Oh thank you!" Angeline squealed in delight and jumped up to hug her parents. "You're both wonderful and I love you so!"

two

For the next few weeks, travel was all that Angeline could speak of. She enthusiastically bought magazines and books, as well as newspapers, all in the hopes of planning an adventure to equal her dreams.

An unexpected damper came upon things when a German submarine torpedoed and sank the British passenger ship Lusitania. The ship was only twelve miles from Irish shores and over eleven hundred people lost their lives. One hundred and twenty-eight of them were Americans. The event caused not only a hush to fall over the country, but from that hush rose up an anguished cry that demanded revenge. Collectively, Americans held their breath waiting to see if their country would break neutrality and join the others already at war.

Angeline saw the worried looks her parents exchanged. They were thinking of her older brothers, John and James, both in the army now. Would they be called to fight in the European War?

Angeline stewed and fretted with everyone else. She teetered on the brink of adulthood, with still very childish theories on how the world really worked. It was beyond her to understand why anyone would kill helpless human beings.

Sunday services were devoted to continued prayer for Europe and the survivors of the Lusitania, along with the fervent hope that America could somehow escape the nightmare. Angeline sat stiffly prim and proper, while Pastor David Monroe, her father's only brother, offered words of encouragement.

"God is with us," David reminded them. "He is watching over and tenderly caring for each and every soul, even as shots are fired in Europe, even as the war rages on. He knows our fears and our heartaches."

Angeline glanced sideways at her parents, who gripped each other's hands tightly. They had each other to comfort and Angeline suddenly felt very alone. Her own fears made her feel very vulnerable and that vulnerability softened her normally controlled expression.

With a look that resembled a frightened child, Angeline noted that her mother had tears in her eyes. Gently, her father reached upward and caught one as it rolled down her cheek. The look he gave his wife, caused Angeline to marvel. They were so in love and so right for one another. Could she ever hope to know that same feeling?

After watching her parents for another moment, Angeline raised her face and locked eyes with Gavin Lucas. He seemed to sense her need and the look he offered gave Angeline a feeling of comfort and peace. Then, just as quickly as it was given, Gavin resumed his study of the Bible in his hands and Angeline was again alone.

First he ignores me, Angeline thought to herself, *and now he acts as though he'd like nothing better than to put an arm around me. What in the world is Gavin thinking?* She continued to contemplate the situation long after Pastor David had directed them to turn to a popular hymn.

❧

Dinner at the Monroe house was quiet and reserved. Angeline hardly felt like eating as she pushed her food around the plate.

"You know what I think," her father began with a cautious glance to Lillie. "I think we need some diversion from all this sorrow." Lillie nodded but said nothing, while Angeline gave her father her undivided attention.

"I learned today that Mrs. Widdle plans a train trip to Denver to see her niece. I took the liberty of speaking with her and suggested that you might accompany her."

Angeline perked up noticeably. "Truly?"

"Yes," Daniel replied. "She seemed quite happy about the idea, in fact. She said that her niece had more than enough room to house you and there would be ample time for you to see the town and visit the shops and museums."

"It sounds wonderful!" Angeline's mind raced with thoughts of what she'd wear. "When do I go and how long will I be gone?"

"Mrs. Widdle plans to leave next Friday. She intends to stay for two weeks and then return in time to head up the Sunday school class graduation ceremonies." Daniel paused. "I know it's not as extensive as you'd like. It certainly isn't New York or California, but I think you will be pleasantly surprised."

Angeline gave her father a reassuring smile. "I know it will be grand!"

Lillie smiled at her daughter. "It will be, but you must be cautious. Denver is a very big city and the likes of which you've never even known. People can't be trusted the way they are here."

"Your mother is right, Angeline. The larger the city, the less personal and more problematic," her father joined in.

"I will be on my guard," Angeline offered, completely unconcerned with her parents' worries. She was going to Denver in less than a week! *Denver!*

&

"She's going to Denver, at least that's what Dr. Dan said," Dolan relayed to Gavin.

"How soon?" he asked trying to sound like it was unimportant. Inside he felt as though someone had dealt his midsection a severe blow.

"I guess she's leaving Friday," Dolan answered. "Aunt Lillie thought it'd be fun to have a little party to send Angeline off on her trip. She told me to be sure and have everybody come over Thursday evening for Angeline's last night in Bandelero. So she must be leaving the next day."

Gavin took in the news and frowned when his brother wasn't looking. This wasn't in his plans and given his serious manner of planning everything out to the last detail, the news was rather upsetting.

"Did you tell Mom?" Gavin finally spoke.

"Not yet, I was just on my way into the house. Hey, you gonna help me unload this feed or just stand there and look like you've lost your last friend?" Gavin gave his younger brother a puzzled look. "Oh, quit trying to play games with me," Dolan smirked. "I know you're in love with Angeline."

"Oh, really?"

Dolan shrugged his shoulders. "It doesn't bother me in the least, although it might be wise to lay your claim to her before she gets all the way to Colorado to look for a husband."

"What makes you think she's going to Colorado to find a husband?" Gavin questioned cautiously. Maybe Angeline had said something to make Dolan believe her interest in matrimonial conquests.

"What else would a woman like Angeline have on her mind?"

Gavin laughed at this. "Knowing Angel, she's got plenty on her mind besides husbands."

Dolan laughed and hoisted a heavy feed sack against Gavin's chest and open arms. "I think you'd better talk to her just the same."

Gavin said nothing but he was still considering Dolan's words an hour later when he saddled up his horse and headed to Bandelero. Maybe it was time to make his intentions clear to Angel. Maybe she was truly too naive to know how he felt. She was, after all, just eighteen.

Gavin rode straight to the Monroe house and noted the absence of the buggy Dr. Dan used for housecalls. With any luck maybe he'd have a chance to talk to Angel, alone.

&

Angeline answered the door with her long blond hair dripping wet. "Gavin!" she exclaimed and quickly threw a towel over her head to hide her hair.

Gavin grinned sheepishly and stuffed his hands deep in his jeans pockets. "You're looking good, Angel."

Angeline blushed crimson. "Mother and Dad are out delivering a baby on the Stanton ranch. Is something wrong?"

"No. I came to see you."

"Me?" Angeline quickly forgot about her appearance, as she lost herself in Gavin's blue-gray eyes.

"May I come in?"

Angeline nodded and stepped back from the door. "I was just washing my hair. If you'll wait in the front room, I need to go comb it out." She wasn't at all the same self-confident girl who usually commanded the attention of everyone around her.

"Why don't you bring your comb and come sit with me?" Gavin's words were soft and alluring.

"I suppose I could," Angeline replied rather nervously. She watched as Gavin made his way through the house, following only a few steps behind before she slipped into her parents' bedroom and retrieved the brush.

Angeline felt a strange sensation ripple through her. It was like a fluttering that started in her stomach and seemed to engulf her entire body. What in the world was wrong with her?

When she appeared in the family sitting room, she held up the brush, momentarily not knowing what else to do. Gavin motioned her to sit and reached out for the brush.

"I think this looks like fun," he said and Angeline was so surprised that she couldn't even protest.

Gavin took the brush in his trembling hands and began to run it down Angeline's long, wet hair. The feeling was like nothing she'd ever known and it was all Angeline could do to remain seated. No one besides her mother had ever brushed her hair and now it seemed that Gavin's actions were the most intimate she'd ever shared with anyone.

Gavin felt the same way, although he, like Angel, would never admit it. Forcing himself to speak, Gavin remembered his brother's words.

"I hear you're taking a trip," he began, "to Denver."

"What?" Angeline's voice gave away her inability to concentrate.

"A trip," Gavin repeated.

"A what?"

Gavin would have enjoyed her reaction had he not felt the same uncertainty and nervousness. "I heard that you planned to visit Denver."

This time Angeline forced herself to ignore the rhythmic stroking and hung on Gavin's every word. "Yes," she managed to reply before losing herself again.

"When are you leaving?"

"Uh. . . Friday. I'm traveling with Mrs. Widdle." Angeline's voice was barely audible.

Gavin continued the long brush strokes. "How long you gonna be gone, Angel?"

"Gone?" she sounded like a child and tried to shake herself out of it. "I'm not sure," she answered. The fact was, she couldn't think clearly and really wasn't sure what her father had said.

Gavin, always given to getting right to the point, stopped in mid-stroke and drew a deep breath. "I came here to talk to you about us."

"Us?" Angeline was hesitant. The single word brought Angeline to complete awareness. "What about us?"

"That's what I want to know."

"I don't guess I understand," Angeline said, turning to face Gavin.

"I don't like the idea of you going off, but I guess it's because I'll miss having you around. It might also be because I don't like the idea of those city fellows giving you ideas and causes that will take you away from here."

Angeline's mouth opened slightly. "What are you saying, Gavin?" she finally asked.

Gavin looked at her for a moment. Her lavender eyes were wide with surprise and even with her hair wet and clinging to her back, Gavin thought she'd never looked more attractive.

"Look, Angel, we've grown up together. There's never been a time when I haven't been a part of your life."

"The same can be said of your brothers and sister, too," Angeline protested. She was quickly beginning to see where Gavin was headed.

"That's true enough," he replied. Pausing for a moment, Gavin put the brush aside and reached out to pull Angeline to her feet. "The fact is, Angel, I've loved you since you were a little girl. I made up my mind when I was sixteen and you were just twelve, that you were the one I intended to marry."

"Marry?" Angeline dropped her hands from Gavin's and took a step backwards. "Marry?"

Gavin smiled. "I think I've been rather patient while you've courted half the town. Now I'm just laying my claim before you go off and get half of Denver to fall in love with you as well."

Angeline was stunned. For all the attention she was used to receiving, no one had ever asked her to marry them. Now here was Gavin Lucas, the one man who seemed least interested in her, and he was proposing marriage. No, he was demanding it, she thought.

Gavin seemed unconcerned with Angeline's shock. "Look Angel," he said stepping towards her, "it's time to consider the future. I want you to be my wife."

Angeline quickly regain her composure and ducked under Gavin's outreaching arms. Putting a chair between them, Angeline shook her head. "I can't believe you think you can just waltz in here and propose like that. Gavin Lucas, I have no intention of marrying you or anyone else!"

Gavin was the one who looked surprised now. Angeline quickly took the advantage. "You've treated me like I have some awful disease these last months. Hardly ever talking to me at parties or picnics. Never so much as saying a single word when we crossed paths in town. Now you come here and tell me that you've chosen me for your wife, like it's some kind of honor."

Gavin grinned at this. "You might consider it just that, after you get the ring on your finger."

Angeline shook her head. "I'm not ready to marry anyone yet."

"You are a bit immature, I'll give you that."

"Why you. . .you," Angeline stammered for something to say.

"Look, Angel," Gavin said easily pushing the chair aside in order to get to the woman he loved. "I know I've surprised you, but it's not like we've never had anything between us."

"What have we had between us, except friendship?"

"Friendship is a good start," Gavin said softly. "But we've always had more than that. You're friends with my brothers too, but I'll wager you don't feel the same things for them that you do for me."

Angeline shook her head once again. "I don't know what you're talking about. I like all of you. You're like family to me. But, I intend to travel a great deal. I want to go abroad when those European ninnies quit fighting with each other. I want to fly in one of those aeroplanes. I want to sail on the ocean and I can't do any of that by getting myself married off to you or anyone else." Angeline noted that Gavin seemed completely unmoved by her declaration. "Besides that, there are things I want to do and be a part of. There are important causes out there, things that I can help with." Angel backed up while Gavin just kept coming toward her. "I mean it, Gavin, I don't have those kind of feelings for you."

Gavin reached out and pulled Angeline into his arms, then very gently he tilted her chin upward and kissed her deeply. Angel was too shocked to do anything. She felt Gavin's strong arms encircle her waist, while his lips commanded her attention.

She held herself rigid, hoping the kiss would end in just a moment, but it didn't. When Gavin continued to kiss her, Angeline couldn't help but feel her resistance give way. It was after all, her first kiss. Although Angeline would never have admitted it to Gavin.

When Gavin felt her stiffness give way, he stopped kissing er abruptly and set Angeline away from him. He grinned when he gripped the back of a near-by chair to steady herself.

Then, completely to Angeline's surprise, Gavin turned and vithout even stopping to look back at her, called out, "I think ou should reconsider what you think you feel, Angel. I have ny own causes and marrying you is right at the top of the st."

three

Thursday evening arrived and Angeline forced thoughts of Gavin from her head and replaced them with ones of the party to come. She dressed carefully in a white gown of cotton eyelet which was trimmed daintily with ribbons of pink. Three flounces fell in graceful swirls to make up the skirt, while the bodice fit snug to accentuate Angeline's small waist. She pulled her hair back from her face and tied part of it with a large pink ribbon that matched those on her dress. Twirling before her mother's chival mirror, Angeline smiled. She'd never looked better and she was more than a little pleased.

Angeline went downstairs and found everyone in a surprisingly good mood. Letters had come that day from John and James, and her mother was greatly relieved to learn that they were well. Her father, one of only two doctors in the town, happily announced that he had successfully saved the leg of one of the town's older residents. The man had taken a fall on his horse, crushing his leg and breaking it in several places. Dr. Monroe had worked most diligently to restore the limb and now after ten days of battling a fierce infection, he declared the leg well on the way to mending. Everyone was happy and the tone of the party was set in that mood.

The first to arrive at the party was David and Jenny Monroe and their twins Samuel and Hannah. At twenty, neither of the twins seemed all that concerned with leaving home. Samuel seemed to favor banking, while Hannah had spent the last year diligently working on the Belgian Relief cause

24

Angeline herself had joined Hannah's efforts for a time, until boredom set in, as it usually did, and she was off and running to right wrongs somewhere else.

Angeline seldom gave too much consideration to her cousins. They were simple people, uninterested in the things that Angeline found fascinating and completely too quiet to be considered fun.

The Lucas' arrived not far behind David and Jenny, and Angeline was relieved when Gavin seemed content to keep his distance and not bring up their previous conversation. Still, Angeline couldn't help but watch Gavin out of the corner of her eye. She felt herself tremble once when she caught him staring at her, but when he did nothing but grin and give her a slight nod, Angeline calmed a bit and chided herself for being silly.

Maybe he's thought better of it, Angeline decided silently. *Maybe he's sorry and embarrassed for asking me to marry him.* But just as soon as she considered that thought, Angeline knew that she didn't want him to be. She rather liked the idea of having been proposed to, although she had no intention of accepting. A woman should be flattered when a handsome young man asked for her hand.

"But he didn't ask," Angeline muttered, quickly looking up to see who else might have overheard her.

"What was that, dear?" her mother questioned, but no one else seemed to have heard.

"Nothing," Angeline said, forcing a smile. "Nothing at all."

❧

The Monroe's beautifully cultivated yard was soon filled with several dozen people. Angeline was pleased with the effort her parents had gone to. Her father had strung paper lanterns round the yard and her mother had decorated a beautiful

buffet of food for all of the guests to enjoy. Angeline ha
never felt so special in all her life.

It didn't take long for the men to begin their courting
Angeline was soon the center of attention, laughing at thei
stories and pretending to be shocked at the risks they faced i
their jobs. But Gavin wasn't among them and for the firs
time, Angeline wasn't nearly as interested in what the othe
men had to say. What was wrong with her?

From time to time, Angeline sought the crowd for Gavin
Inevitably, she found him after searching for several minutes
only to realize that he knew, when their eyes met, that she'
been looking for him. He'd smile smugly, maybe give her
nod, but otherwise he made no attempt to command her at
tention or greet her. Angeline felt a sense of ineffable disap
pointment when Gavin finally turned to engage in conversa
tion with Hannah and Samuel.

&

An hour or so later, the party seemed to be dying down an
Angeline knew everyone would make their way back home
She felt a sense of loss and didn't know why. She was goin
to Denver to see and do wonderful new things. Why shoul
she feel this way now?

Looking at her daughter from a distance, Lillie couldn'
help but wonder what was going on in Angeline's mind. Sh
sported the semblance of contentment, Lillie thought, but sh
couldn't really be sure. Angeline was harder to understand i
some ways and in others, Lillie thought she knew her as inti
mately as she knew herself.

It was while watching Angeline that Lillie's eyes drifte
past the crowd of encircling admirers to where Gavin Luca
stood alone. He was a handsome boy and so industrious. I
many ways, he reminded her of her youngest son, James. The

had been good friends, almost inseparable at times, and very nearly the same age. Lillie remembered fondly when she and Maggie Lucas had shared their expectations for the babes to come and how much fun it had been to plan and dream together. Making her way to him, Lillie wasn't surprised to find Gavin's attention focused on Angeline.

"Sometimes I think she's too popular," Lillie said, coming to stand beside Gavin.

"She deserves to enjoy herself," Gavin replied softly.

"Still, a mother worries about such things. Angeline is very stubborn, like her father," Lillie said with a grin that Gavin shared.

"I heard tell it was the other way around," Gavin offered lightly. "In fact, I've heard a few stories about you and my mom that make Angel seem kind of tame."

Lillie laughed out loud. "Gavin Lucas you've been listening to your father again. Or was it Daniel?"

"Both," Gavin admitted. "I guess they just want to train me up so I'll not be shocked when I take a wife."

"Then your mother and I had best get busy and give you our side," Lillie said with genuine affection for Gavin. She looped her arm through his and with a more motherly tone, spoke of courtship. "Stubbornness can be both a virtue and a curse, depending on how you use it. In my case, stubbornness keeps Dr. Dan and I together. But, we love each other a great deal," she added softly, "and just like the Bible says in Proverbs ten, verse twelve, 'Love covereth all sins.'"

"It does tend to make you overlook things, doesn't it?" Gavin reflected, his eyes still on Angeline.

Lillie was rather taken back by his response. She followed his gaze to her daughter. "I worry something fierce about her, Gavin. She's so young and she's not a bit aware of how ugly the world can really be. Now she's going off to Denver and after that, who knows where? Her heart is so soft and giving, and she'll expect everyone else to be the same way." Lillie stopped, pulled her arm from Gavin's, and realized her heart was much heavier than she knew.

Silence engulfed them for a moment and then Gavin turned to his mother's lifelong friend. "Don't worry about Angel," he said softly. "I intend to see to it that she's well cared for. I'll never let anyone hurt her if I'm able to do anything about it."

Lillie smiled at Gavin's chivalrous reply. "You can't be everywhere, Gavin. Angeline's bound to take wings and fly away someday and there's no way I can stop that. Not that I really want to stop her from growing up, it's just that I worry about the kind of people she'll meet; the type of man she'll finally settle down to marry."

"Then stop worrying about it," Gavin said boldly. "I intend to marry Angel and I told her so. She just needs to get used to the idea."

Lillie's mouth dropped open at Gavin's declaration. "You what?"

Gavin looked a bit embarrassed as if suddenly realizing was Angel's mother he was talking to. "I hope that didn't seem too out of place. I do intend to speak with Dr. Daniels about it before just barging into the family."

Lillie was still dumbstruck. He was serious. Gavin Lucas intended to marry her daughter! There was no chance to further the conversation, however, because Garrett and Maggie came up to announce they were heading for home.

"I'll help you get the wagon," Gavin said to his father and followed him off into the night.

"I've certainly enjoyed myself," Maggie said, then nodded

wards Angeline. "Looks like she has, as well."

"Yes," Lillie replied and looked at where Gavin had stood
ly minutes before. Should she say something to Maggie?
aybe she should asked her how she felt about them finally
ing joined as in-laws?

"The children always seem to love these get togethers. I
ish Daughtry lived closer. I miss her so much when she's
ne and it seems like when she and Nicholas come for a
sit, all we do is talk about Kent and what new thing he's
ing. I never seem to get to talk about what she's doing or
nking."

"I know what you mean and I have Angeline here all the
ne. It just seems as if she's drifting away. Did you know
at she wants to travel abroad?"

"Not a healthy time to do that," Maggie replied.

"No, but she reminds me so much of myself. Remember
nen I nagged my mother into taking me to London?"

"Do I ever! I was green with envy."

Lillie nodded. "Now it's our children. Now, instead of
ngs happening to us, it's them. Doesn't that seem strange?"

Maggie laughed. "It does indeed. I remember thinking
nen Daughtry was expecting Kent that it used to be me bring-
g the new lives into our family. All of the sudden, I changed
ices with my child and she was a child no more."

"Yes, that's it," Lillie said as though the thought were a
velation. "I felt that way tonight, almost as if I were an
tsider looking in." Lillie's words were a puzzle to Maggie
d her expression told her friend so. "I used to be that young
ly," Lillie said pointing to her daughter.

"Yes, I remember you telling me all about it," Maggie
reed.

"You'd never come to the parties because you were sworn

to never marry." Lillie couldn't help but laugh. "Now, ju
look at you."

"God had other plans," Maggie replied softly. "I thank Hi
too, that He did."

"The same goes for me," Lillie happily seconded. The
completely changing the subject, she reached out and too
hold of Maggie's hand. "Gavin is so much like Garrett. He
a good man, as are all of your sons."

Maggie's eyes narrowed at Lillie's sudden praise. "Wh
is it?" she questioned. "What are you trying to say to me?"

Lillie looked across the short distance to Angeline, the
back to Maggie. "Gavin told me tonight that he intends
marry Angeline." Maggie's mouth dropped open in surpris
"He told me not to worry about her," Lillie continued, "b
cause he intends to take care of her."

"Well, I'll be." Maggie finally breathed the words. S
couldn't help but get a get a mischievous look to her fac
"His brothers will never let him hear the end of it for th
Has he asked Angeline yet?"

"I think so, but he said she needed time to get used to t
idea."

Maggie laughed heartily. "Sounds like his father. Pc
Angeline."

Lillie smirked a grin as she glanced at her daughter. "Pc
Gavin."

four

ngeline returned home from Denver a changed woman. Her
cabulary was expanded to include words like suffrage, fran-
ise, and equal rights. Furthermore, she now quoted women
o had made their marks in history—Susan B. Anthony,
rrie Chapman Catt, Alice Paul, and Elizabeth Cady Stanton,
name a few. In short, Angeline had a new cause. Women's
ffrage! The right to vote!

"Mother, you wouldn't believe what I learned," Angeline
mbled in animated excitement. "Colorado agreed in 1893
allow their women to vote and Wyoming even entered the
ion fully granting suffrage rights to their women!"

Lillie took it all in stride. Angeline was always at one cause
another. It was really a small wonder she hadn't been
tten by the suffrage bug sooner. It wasn't until Angeline
nounced her plan to join the suffragist Willa Neal on her
cture tour through New Mexico that Lillie stopped dead in
r tracks.

"You what?"

"Oh, Mother," Angeline's voice oozed excitement, "I'm
ing to fight for the suffrage cause! I'm going to be a suf-
agist and win us the right to vote!"

Lillie eyed her daughter carefully. "Angeline, we need to
scuss this more thoroughly with your father. I doubt he'll
very enthusiastic to the idea of you traipsing off with strang-
s."

"It won't be the idea of strangers that will bother him. He'll

31

be narrow-minded like most men and not see a need for wom[en] to vote."

"Angeline, I don't care for your tone. When has your f[a]ther ever given you cause to believe that he doesn't esteem [a] woman's opinion?" Lillie asked her daughter in genuine co[n]cern. Who had put such ideas into her little girl's head?

"Mother," Angeline began very patiently, as though s[he] were talking to a simpleton or small child, "women have be[en] made to believe for a very long time that they were incapa[ble] of sound judgement. We marry and give birth to men, ra[ise] them to adulthood, but somehow when it comes to logic a[nd] sense, men believe us totally null and void—completely [un]educated and without a hope of making responsible decision[s]. Yet who do they think trained them up? On who's knee [did] they learn their first words?"

Lillie stared at her daughter in complete shock. Angeli[ne] seemed unconcerned with her mother's surprise. It was to [be] expected, she reasoned. Hadn't Willa told her that wom[en] were as much to blame, maybe even more so, for their ow[n] lack of rights?

"Mother, this is a new age and the men and women of t[he] world need to wake up to the realization that the world [is] growing up and moving on." Angeline voiced the practic[al] words she'd heard at one of the many suffrage lectures sh[e] attended in Denver. "We have the automobiles being ma[ss] produced on an assembly line where workers are paid fi[ve] dollars a week! There are aeroplanes that fly men in the [air] and moving pictures that can record things as they happ[en]. And with all this technology and progress toward a bet[ter] world, woman are still suppressed and treated as though th[ey] are second class citizens!"

"Enough!" Lillie cried and put her hands on her hi[ps]

"Angeline, I'm happy to know that you spent your time learning about the world, but honestly, you rant this suffrage cause like you had been made to endure some horrendous ordeal. Your father and brothers have only treated us with the utmost of respect. Your father, a college trained doctor, often seeks my opinion in cases of his female patients, simply because I am a woman. You have only known kindness and respect from the men in this community and I resent the fact that you act as though it has been otherwise."

Angeline was taken back by her mother's outrage. "While it is true," Angeline countered, "that our menfolks have offered certain deference to our opinions, they still see us as frail, weak creatures who need to be sheltered from the pains of the world."

"I don't think I understand why you feel this way," Lillie said a bit softer.

Angeline came to her mother and took hold of her hands. "Mother, you wouldn't believe the things that are done to women, everyday all over the world. Women, who because they have no voice and no chance to make changes, are put upon to be all manner of things for all manner of men. Some are bought and sold for the pleasure of others and when they dare to raise a hand in their own defense they are maimed and often murdered!"

Lillie sat down at her kitchen table, pulling Angeline with her to take the chair beside hers. "Angeline, I know full well of the ugliness in this world. I have chosen not to make it an issue in your upbringing because I hoped I could shelter you from it for as long as possible. Perhaps it was naive of me. Perhaps it was unwise, but nevertheless, it had nothing to do with equal rights and whether women should or shouldn't have the right to vote."

Angeline took in her mother's words and weighed them against her new found knowledge. "I didn't mean to sound harsh," Angeline began, "but Willa Neal told me that often women are a worse enemy to our cause than men."

"You mean she doesn't get the reaction she wants from women and so she calls them an enemy?"

"No, of course not!" Angeline exclaimed. "She simply means that sometimes women are too misinformed and need to be educated."

"Sounds like the same argument you told me that men give for why they won't approve women's rights to vote."

Angeline was temporarily silenced at her mother's logical argument. Finally, she decided she needed to put the conversation on a more positive track and switched to another related, but seemingly neutral topic. "I did so enjoy being around learned women, Mother. I always knew that you and Aunt Jenny and Maggie were women of knowledge, but these women have attended college and they seem to know so much."

Lillie didn't know quite what to say. She realized Angeline's change in tactics, but feared her daughter's vulnerability to these "learned women." "Wisdom is a powerful thing, Angeline. Solomon was wise and he still struggled to make the proper judgments."

"Proverbs seven, verse four says, 'Say unto wisdom, Thou art my sister; and call understanding thy kinswoman.' Willa told this to me, Mother. God, Himself, gave a clear picture that wisdom is a feminine virtue."

"Is that all you perceive in that verse? Did you pay any attention to what came before it or went after it? You can't rip pieces out of the Bible to fit your causes, Angeline."

Angeline seemed genuinely deflated and Lillie felt sorry

for her daughter. "Look, I would very much like the right to vote." Angeline perked up at this declaration, but Lillie waved her into silence and continued. "However, I will not fight a cause that degrades the rights of one to boost the rights of another. Nor will I see God's hand in a fight that leads people into civil disobedience and self-declared war against one another."

Daniel chose that inopportune moment to come whistling through the back door entrance. Lillie fell silent as she heard Daniel cast aside his doctor's bag. Entering the kitchen, Daniel noted the stern expression on his wife's face and an even more troubling look of composed anger on his daughter's.

"What are you two arguing about this time?" Dan asked seriously.

Lillie got up and went to embrace her husband, while Angeline stood and waited by the table. "It seems," Lillie told Daniel softly, "Angeline wants to accompany a leading suffragist on her lecture circuit."

Daniel grinned. "Suffrage, eh?" He looked at his daughter with genuine affection, but she saw it as a patronizing gesture.

"I know what both of you are thinking and you're wrong!" Angeline declared. "I believe in this cause and I intend to fight it for all I'm worth. I may not be old enough to benefit from it yet, but in a few years I'll be twenty-one and then I'll be able to hold my head up high on the way to the voting place."

"Whoa, Angeline," Daniel said, stepping away from his wife. "There's no reason for you to get so upset."

"You and Mother think I'm a child," Angeline protested, "but I'm not. I'm a grown woman and I have rights and I intend to fight for those rights. Willa Neal is a wonderful

woman. She has a great deal of knowledge and she's gradu-
ated from a very fine college back east." She paused long
enough to point a finger at her mother. "And while I might
have expected this from Father, I thought you would understand. But I see you're just as misinformed and naive as
Willa said most women are." Turning to leave, Angeline
paused at the door. "I believe in this cause and I believe what
she says in regards to what needs to be done. With or without
your permission, I intend to join her."

Daniel's face changed instantly from compassionate to
fiercely stern. "That's enough, Angeline. You'll do no such
thing, until we deem it acceptable and in your best interest.
Now, apologize to your mother."

Angeline turned up her nose and stormed from the room.
There was no way she intended to apologize. Not when she
was right!

Feeling very much the martyr, Angeline threw herself across
her bed and pounded the mattress in rage. Willa had warned
her that this would happen and Angeline hadn't believe it
possible. Was the entire world blind to the needs of women?

৵

Lillie's astounded expression exactly matched her husband's.
When Daniel opened his arms to her, Lillie eagerly sought
the refuge he offered.

"She's so different now," Lillie said near to tears. "I thought
maybe we could talk through it, but she just kept getting more
upset with each thing I said."

"Shhh," Daniel soothed. "It has nothing to do with you."

"She thinks I'm stupid," Lillie said and a sob escaped her.
"Stupid and oppressed and blind to my womanly rights."

Daniel smiled over his wife's head. "Yeah, you seem real
oppressed, Lillie. Have I managed to keep you chained to my

side, unable to achieve your God-given potential?"

Lillie pulled back and looked at the amused twinkle in her husband's eye. "Oh, Daniel," she grinned and wiped at the tears in her eyes, "I'll take oppression if it's with you."

Daniel took Lillie's face in his hands and kissed her soundly on the lips. "I feel the same way about you, my dear."

Lillie melted against her husband, perfectly content that after twenty-some years of marriage, they could still argue together, work together, and joyfully love together. They had weathered many storms and would undoubtably face many more.

"What are we going to do about Angeline?" Lillie whispered the question against Daniel's chest.

"Give her time to cool off and come to her senses. Maybe she'll get interested in one of the local causes and forget about her suffragist friend."

"I suppose you're right," Lillie said wrapping her arms tightly around Daniel's neck. "I hope you are."

"If not, there's always my idea about a convent."

&

Angeline's tantrum was spent and now she felt more determined than ever to leave Bandelero and assist Miss Neal. She pulled out a calendar and noted the day when Willa planned to be in Santa Fe for her first speech. With any luck at all, Angeline would find a way to join her.

"I'll show them that I'm more than a simple-minded female," Angeline whispered to the room. "I'll show them that I'm capable of bettering the cause for women! I'll show them all!"

&

For the next few days, Angeline was the epitome of cooperation and genteel refinement. She didn't utter a single word about suffrage or equal rights and went about her chores as a dutiful daughter. She was content in the fact that no one was wise to her plans. She reasoned away any feelings of guilt, telling herself that even people in the Bible often had to step out of line in order to accomplish God's will.

On what was to be her last evening at home, Angeline sat quietly sewing while her father discussed one of his cases. Her mother was quite engrossed in the conversation, adding her own thoughts on Daniel's procedures. All in all, Angeline thought it a perfect evening. It was the way she wanted to remember her parents. It was the way she wanted to remember her home.

Getting up and excusing herself for bed, Angeline went to her room and double-checked her suitcase. Everything was ready. She opened her window and cautiously lowered her case to the ground by using a rope she'd managed to hide beneath her bed. Then securing that same rope to the leg of her bed, Angeline prepared to descend in the same manner.

She cast a quick look around the room and smiled. She was leaving a child, but when she returned, if she returned, she'd be a worldly, wise woman. She double-checked to make certain they would see her letter of explanation, then pulled on her jacket and hat, and climbed out her bedroom window.

Reaching the ground, Angeline heard the train whistle blast it's announcement that final boarding was taking place. She picked up the suitcase and ran for all she was worth, managing to pat her pocket and reassure herself that her ticket and money were both still within.

She approached the train depot cautiously, for the first time worried that someone might see her and try to stop her. Thoughts of Gavin came to mind more than once. She'd only been home for four days and no doubt Gavin planned to see her Sunday at church. Poor Gavin would be so surprised, she thought and stepped up onto the traincar's platform. They would all be surprised, she smiled as she took her seat.

five

Angeline was filled with anticipation as she rode away from Bandelero. The adventure of what she was doing made her giddy and she couldn't help but succumb to her own joy.

"I'm really doing it!" she whispered, staring out into the pitch blackness of the night.

In spite of her excitement, the gentle rocking of the train against the rails made Angeline sleepy and without meaning to, she slipped into a deep, dreamless sleep.

"Miss, this is your stop," a gentle voice was calling to her.

Angeline sat up with a start and immediately winced at the stiffness in her neck. She looked up into the face of the conductor and nodded rigidly. "Thank you," she offered and glanced out the window into the predawn.

"Do you have folks to meet you?" the man asked her.

"No," Angeline responded as if it was unimportant. "I'm catching the southbound train to Santa Fe later this morning."

"Well, you'll have a bit of a wait," the man offered.

Somehow, Angeline hadn't considered this possibility. "I'll be fine," she said with a false sense of courage. Taking her case in hand, Angeline followed the man down the aisle and allowed him to assist her from the train.

"You can wait in the depot," he suggested. "At least the ticket agent will be nearby, if anyone tries to bother you."

"Thank you," Angeline replied and made her way into the dimly lit building.

The room was seemingly deserted and Angeline swallowed hard to keep her nerve. She made her way slowly to a long empty bench and took a seat with a wary glance into the shadowy corners. She clutched her suitcase close and thought to whisper a prayer.

She stopped however before uttering the words. Would God listen to her? She was, after all, disobeying her parents, but wasn't that a verse for children? Didn't God intend that to be a guidance for when you were young and didn't know how to care for yourself? Deciding that she was completely within her rights, Angeline offered a simple prayer and waited impatiently for time to pass.

&

When the Santa Fe train finally pulled along side the depot, Angeline was exhausted and hungry. She made her way slowly to the train, wondering how in the world she would find Willa, but to her surprise, Willa found her instead.

"Angeline!" the older woman cried from the platform.

"Am I ever glad to see you!" Angeline replied.

Willa Neal was a rather severe looking woman. Nearing her forty-fifth birthday, she was the very image of cartoon depictions of suffragists. Although, as Willa had already shown Angeline, the newspaper cartoons were much kinder to the suffragists these days than they had been twenty or so years earlier.

Dressed in her plain brown skirt and jacket, Willa had pulled her mousy brown hair back into a tight bun, without so much as a single wisp to escape the dourness. In actuality, she might have been a pleasant enough looking woman had she styled her hair differently and wore more flattering clothes. But, looking nice was not a concern of Willa Neal. Suffrage was! Suffrage was all she would give her precious efforts to.

"I'm glad you decided to join us, Angeline," Willa said leading Angeline down the aisle of the train car. "Did you have any difficulty in winning your parents to our cause?"

"Yes," Angeline replied rather curtly. "I had a great deal of trouble. In fact, they didn't want me to accompany you."

"Typical!" Willa expressed with a nod. "Well, I'm glad you used the brains the good Lord gave you and came along anyway. Look here, there's someone I want you to meet." Angeline lifted her face to meet the gaze of a very handsome man. "Angeline Monroe, this is Douglas Baker. He is a great help to our cause and politically aligned to do us much good. He is very ambitious and very well may one day be President of the United States."

Angeline couldn't hide her surprise as she extended her hand to the gentleman before her. Bending over and lifting Angeline's hand to his lips, Douglas Baker kissed the back very gently, then lifted his head to reveal a broad smile. "I am charmed."

Angeline stared long and hard into the most beautiful green eyes she'd ever seen. Douglas Baker was very nearly perfect, she concluded. She pulled back her hand reluctantly and offered a weak version of her own smile. "How do you do?"

"Quite well," he replied, straightening up again. "In fact, much better now that you are a part of our entourage."

Willa laughed. "Douglas is quite the flatterer. He specializes in making women swoon and babies laugh."

"What about the men?" Angeline questioned without giving it any thought.

"I out-smart the men," Douglas answered with a mischievous smile. "Those I can't out-smart, well," he paused and laughed, "I guess I haven't run across that man yet."

Angeline enjoyed his banter and took the window seat that

Willa directed her to. Douglas quickly possessed the seat directly across from Angeline, while Willa sat beside her.

Angeline couldn't help but stare at Douglas. He was the kind of man who demanded attention and drew it to himself when it was otherwise unoffered. He was of average height and not nearly as muscular as Gavin, Angeline decided. But, he was more stately in his appearance and his neatly manicured hands indicated he spent most of his time behind a desk instead of outdoors.

Willa began speaking before the train even pulled out of the station and Douglas was happy to engage the older woman in debates regarding the suffrage movement. Angeline simply sat back and took it all in. Mostly, she watch Douglas, fascinated with the way he conducted himself. She was so engrossed in her study of his neatly parted blond hair, that she missed hearing the question that Willa posed.

"I'm sorry," Angeline said, blushing slightly. "What did you say?"

Willa seemed oblivious to the reason Angeline had missed her question, but Douglas wasn't. He gave Angeline a sly wink, nearly causing her to miss Willa's repeated words.

"I was curious as to whether you were acquainted with anyone in the Santa Fe area?"

Angeline nodded. "Yes, I know several families there." She hadn't really considered it before, but she quickly added up at least a dozen or more names who were not only acquainted with her family, but actively involved in the government.

"It always helps to get local cooperation," Willa stated. She knew she would need to ease Angeline into the game of using political association to further the cause. Angeline had no way of knowing, of course, but Willa had already thoroughly checked the young girl out. It was with great pleasure

that Willa learned the Monroe family shared many close tie
to some of the political giants in New Mexico's three-year
old state government. Giants, who had welded the power tha
brought the territory to statehood and now could very wel
bring suffrage to their state as well.

"I haven't seen some of them for a very long time, but man
of the families that come to mind are close friends of my par
ents or at very least, associates of my father, who is a physi
cian."

"Good, good," Willa said and nodded toward Douglas
"Perhaps you will have the opportunity to introduce Dougla
as well. He speaks the language of bureaucrats and often ca
sway them to listen to our cause."

"Do you out-smart them?" Angeline asked with a shy smile

"Of course," Douglas replied candidly. "In politics it i
required to stay two steps ahead of your opponent."

"But what of your allies?" Angeline questioned.

"Ahh," Douglas grinned, "for allies, it's best to stay fiv
steps ahead and two steps behind."

Angeline giggled, while Willa nodded as though Dougla
had spoken a profound truth.

❧

Angeline soon found it necessary to excuse herself and onc
she was gone from the room Willa Neal leaned forward
"What do you think?" she asked in a whisper.

"I think she's incredibly young," Douglas replied gravely
"She's not even old enough to vote, even if she had that righ
Are you sure we won't have her parents chasing after us an
putting out warning bells to prevent her from accompanyin
us?"

"I've thought of that, but from all indications Angelin
seems quite capable of getting her own way. My sources te

he she's the only child at home and the only girl in the family. I'll encourage her to call home and smooth matters over r at least to telegram."

"You'd better hope she has the connections you're looking or," Douglas said, easing back into his seat. "It won't do uch good to have her tagging along if she can't get us the udience we need."

"She will," Willa replied confidently. "She's putty in my ands. I'll have no difficulty in controlling her."

"Has she any clue that you're using her?"

"Why, Mr. Baker, whatever do you mean?"

Douglas chuckled to himself and very nearly sneered at the lder woman. "You know perfectly well what I mean, but ince I'm using you as much as you're using her, I guess I /on't protest too much."

Willa's normally stern expression broke into a smug look f satisfaction. "That's good of you, Douglas. Very good of ou, indeed."

ò

ngeline returned to find Douglas and Willa pleasantly chatng about the barren New Mexico scenery. "I'm positively amished," she said, taking her seat. "Might I dare to hope at there's a dining car on this train?"

"There is indeed and one of the best," Douglas said with ormal bravado. "Perhaps you would allow me to escort you vely ladies to breakfast?"

Angeline glanced at Willa who shook her head. "I'm not ungry, but you two go on ahead."

"Are you certain?" Angeline questioned her mentor.

"Absolutely. Besides, why would you want an old woman ke me along? This handsome young pup hasn't taken his yes off you since you've boarded the train. It will do you

good to get to know an educated man of Douglas' back-
ground." Willa's words caused Angeline to blush.

"Don't mind her," Douglas said, tucking Angeline's arm
around his own. "Willa's a very smart woman," he added
with a smile over Angeline's head at the older woman. "Very
smart."

૨૦

Breakfast was a pleasant affair and Angeline was almost sorry
to see it end. She followed Douglas down the narrow train
aisle on the way back to their car and found herself righted
by his strong arm when the train suddenly lurched.

"You must always be prepared," Douglas said with a smile.
His hand firmly held her at the elbow and Angeline couldn'
help but gaze deep into his green eyes.

"Prepared?" she whispered, completely captivated by the
man's charismatic appeal.

"Yes." He was already much too close, but if possible he
leaned in even closer. "All battles are won with concentrated
effort going into preparation."

"Oh," Angeline managed to say, before Douglas pulled
away with a dashing grin and another quick wink.

"I think I shall enjoy teaching you the game," Douglas re
marked before once again moving down the aisle.

"No more than I shall playing it," Angeline muttered to
herself with a smile.

૨૦

"Here you are," Willa said, waiting for Angeline to take her
seat. "I was beginning to wonder if I'd lost you to Douglas
wily ways."

Angeline looked from Douglas to Willa and shook her head
"No, I just like to eat a lot." At this Willa joined Douglas
laugh with her own.

"It doesn't seem to have hurt you any," Willa finally said. She shifted in her seat to face Angeline. "I have something very exciting to talk to you about. Something I've been considering while you were gone."

"What is it?" Angeline questioned cautiously. She was still uncertain of what Willa Neal expected of her as a traveling companion.

"When we are finished in Santa Fe and the other towns on the lecture circuit, I thought you might accompany me to Washington D.C." Angeline's eyes widened but she said nothing. "We have a meeting with President Wilson and we plan to stage a rally and march to the Capitol."

"How exciting!" Angeline gasped, envisioning the possibility of being a part of the event.

"Then you would consider going with me?"

"Of course," Angeline replied, deeply touched that Willa would ask. "I would be honored." Then realizing it might be difficult to arrange, should her parents decide to interfere, Angeline added, "I will, of course, have to think about it and know more about the preparations." She dared a glance at Douglas knowing she'd find his smile at her choice of words.

Willa nodded completely unconcerned. "Of course. I wouldn't have it any other way."

six

"I can't believe that she defied us and went anyway!" Dani(
bellowed after reading Angeline's letter. "It's the new wa
people look at things these days. Corruption of values ar
such." He was storming through the house, following Lill
whose red-rimmed eyes told the rest of the story.

"I'm going after her and that's that," Daniel said, consi(
erably less noisy than before. He reached out and touche
Lillie's quaking form and pulled her into his arms. "Ah, swe(
heart," he sighed against her carefully pinned hair, "it'll t
alright. I'll find her."

Lillie composed herself for a moment and turned to fac
her husband. "You're needed here," she whispered. "Y(
know half the town doesn't yet trust young Dr. MacGregg(
You can't just break their confidence and leave them to fen
for themselves."

"I can't let Angeline just gallivant around the country lil
she owns the place either." The irritation in Daniel's voi(
was clear. "What in the world ever got into her anyway? W
raised her to know better than to run off with strangers."

"It's her love of causes," Lillie offered. "Her desperate ne(
to right wrongs. In some ways, I admire her gumption and
other ways, she terrifies me."

"Well," Daniel said setting Lillie from him, "I'm going
terrify her when I manage to locate her."

Lillie reached a hand out to stop Daniel from leaving. "The
is another way," she said softly.

48

Daniel turned and eyed her suspiciously. "You're not going to suggest we let her have her way, are you?"

"No, never that," Lillie replied. She thought back to the night of Lillie's going away party and smiled. "I don't suppose Gavin Lucas has had a chance to speak with you, has he?"

"Gavin? No, I haven't talked to him since the party." Daniel looked even more perplexed. "Why would Gavin need to speak with me?"

"Gavin Lucas intends to make Angeline his wife." Lillie stated the words so matter-of-factly that Daniel could only stare back in surprise. "And, I do believe the boy, or should I say young man, is quite determined to do just that. He did, of course, intend to discuss the matter with you first."

Daniel's face erupted in a broad smile. "Gavin and Angeline?"

Lillie smiled and nodded. "He said she just needed time to get used to the idea."

"So he has asked her?"

"That was rather what I gathered," Lillie said and drew Daniel with her to the sofa. "I say, we send for Gavin and if his father can spare him from the ranch, we send him for Angeline."

Daniel's smile broadened. "That would serve her right."

"Better still, I have no doubt that Gavin could get the job done. He has a vested interest and I must say, I haven't seen such determination in a young man since," Lillie paused for a moment and reached up to run her hand through her husband's gray-gold hair, "you decided to pursue me."

"Me?" Daniel pretended to be surprised. "I seem to recall it was you who chased after me. With a frying pan, if I remember correctly."

Lillie remembered the scene in her mind. She had gone to New Mexico to visit Garrett and Maggie. It had been her hope to find some quiet place to think through her life, but that was not to be the case. One Dr. Daniel Monroe was already a house guest at the Lucas ranch and Lillie had endured a rather ugly meeting with him, before even arriving at the ranch.

Throughout their weakly established acquaintance, Daniel had teased her unmercifully about her eating habits. Habits that had led her to a frightful weight gain and deep depression. On the evening in question, Lillie had simply had enough. She picked up a frying pan and ran after Daniel with the serious intention of putting it to the side of his head.

Of course, matters had been made worse when Garrett and Maggie arrived home and found her chasing after Daniel, who was nearly hysterical from her antics.

Lillie snuggled up close, the memory fading in the intensity of her husband's questioning look. "You deserved that frying pan."

Daniel laughed. "Just like Angeline deserves a good spanking."

"I believe she's a little old for that, but," Lillie said with an impish grin, "she's just the right age for a husband."

"Gavin Lucas, eh?" Daniel settled back as if considering the matter. "I'd like to have Gavin for a son. He's a good man and a hard worker and I can't imagine anyone I'd rather have for in-laws than Maggie and Garrett."

"Me, either."

"Angeline will be hard to convince," Daniel said as if this would be news to his wife.

"I'm sure Gavin will have his own way of convincing her."

"You still have that frying pan?"

Lillie laughed and edged her elbow into Daniel's ribs. "Of course. I have to keep it handy just in case."

ᘍ

Gavin Lucas was a little bit surprised when he received a note urging him to come at once to Dan and Lillie's. He immediately feared that something was wrong with Angeline. She'd only been home a few short days and he'd purposefully made himself wait until Sunday to see her.

Leaving word with his brother Jordy, Gavin saddled his horse and road off for Bandelero. On the way, he reconsidered the situation and a more pleasant thought crossed his mind. Maybe Angeline had realized that she loved him and she wanted to tell him that she would marry him. With that thought in mind, Gavin picked up speed, mindless of the hot summer sun blazing down on him.

ᘍ

"Gavin," Lillie said in greeting, "please come in and thank you for being so quick."

"Is something wrong?" Gavin lost his sense of hopeful expectation and replaced it with a nagging dread.

"Nothing we hope you can't help to right," Lillie said. She untied and laid aside her apron and motioned Gavin to follow her. "Come have some coffee with us and we'll explain."

Gavin went with Lillie to the family's favorite gathering room and began to feel rather nervous when Lillie told him to wait there. She left the room, leaving Gavin to battle the butterflies in his stomach. What was going on? Where was Angeline?

"Gavin!" Dan came into the room, with Lillie and a tray of goodies right behind him. "Thanks for coming."

"Sure thing Dr. Dan," Gavin replied.

"Come on and sit down," Daniel motioned. "We have a

great deal to discuss."

Gavin nodded and took the seat Angeline's father offered him. Lillie placed the tray on the coffee table in front of him and took the seat directly opposite, while Daniel chose to stand.

"I'm going to come right to the point, son." Gavin nodded and waited for Daniel to continue. "Lillie tells me that you hope to marry our daughter."

Gavin swallowed hard. "I intended to talk to you first."

"I know you did," Daniel nodded, trying to put Gavin at ease. "Now before you go getting all worried, I want you to know I like the idea. Not only do I like it, I couldn't have chosen better for Angeline, if I'd been given that right."

Gavin physically let out a sigh of relief, causing Lillie to smile sympathetically. "Did you think we were going to roast you over hot coals?"

Gavin smiled. "I was ready for just about anything."

"Good," Daniel said before Lillie could reply, "because we have a problem."

"I suppose Angeline's in the middle of it," Gavin surmised.

"No," Daniel replied. "She is the whole problem."

Gavin grinned at his father's best friend. In all the world, Garrett Lucas had told his son, there was no better man than Daniel Monroe. "Go on," Gavin urged.

"Angeline has run away," Daniel began. "She got it in her mind to join the Women's Suffrage Movement and travel the country whistlestopping and stumping for equal rights and the vote."

Gavin shook his head. "Angel does enjoy her causes."

"That's not the half of it," Lillie joined in. "We forbid her to go. We tried to reason with her and thought we'd made her see our side of it, but last night, she sneaked out of the house and caught the train for Springer. From there she plans to travel south to Santa Fe with a suffragist named Willa Neal."

"What do you want me to do?" Gavin asked coming to the edge of his seat. He hoped Dan and Lillie's words would affirm what he already had in mind.

"We'd like for you to go after her," Daniel said solemnly. "We'd of course pay your expenses."

"No need for that," Gavin said getting to his feet. "I was serious about marrying Angel. I know she cares for me the same way I care for her. But, she's also young and stubborn. This time, though, she may well have gotten herself into more trouble than she can handle."

"Our thoughts exactly," Daniel concurred. "I don't care what it takes, I just want her back here safe and sound. From that point we'll just have to take it day by day."

Lillie reached out and poured a cup of coffee. "Why don't you have some," she said, extending the cup to Gavin.

"No thank you, Aunt Lillie," he said, knowing that one day he would call her by another name. That was, if he could find Angeline before she caused herself harm. Then, he'd have to somehow convince her to marry him, but that was all immaterial at this point.

"I'll need to go home first," he said, already heading for the door. "My folks will need to know what I'm up to."

Lillie and Daniel followed him. "Of course," they said in unison.

Gavin turned at the door. "Try not to worry. Angeline's stubborn, but she's got a good head on her shoulders."

"Thank you, Gavin," Lillie said, reaching out to hug the stern faced young man.

"I'll get her back," he whispered for her ears only and Lillie hugged him even tighter.

"I know you will."

&

Gavin found a captive audience when he returned to the ranch. Maggie and Garrett immediately sensed the urgency in their son and shooed his brothers from the room in order to privately speak with their eldest.

"Is something wrong?" Maggie asked, the worry clearly written in her eyes.

"Yeah," Gavin said with a nod, "it seems Angel has run off to join the Suffrage Movement." Maggie and Garrett both looked rather surprised before Gavin continued. "Lillie and Dan want me to go after her and I told them I would."

Garrett grinned at his wife, who'd already told him that their son intended to marry their best friends' daughter. "Bet that was a hard decision to make."

Gavin couldn't help but flush a bit. "Who told you?"

Maggie laughed out loud at the look of surprise on her son's face. She reached out and rumpled his hair as she'd done when he was a small child. "Does it matter? Do you mind us knowing that you're in love with Angeline?"

Gavin shook his head, then rolled his eyes heavenward. "Please tell me they don't know," he moaned, motioning in the direction Maggie had sent his brothers.

Garrett fairly howled at his son's grim expression. "Gavin, my son, you are the oldest boy and therefore the first to experience the ribbing and teasing that your brother's will goodnaturedly dish out. But, just remind them," Garrett added with a wink, "their time will come and the shoe will be ever so neatly on the other foot."

Gavin smiled, just a bit. It really didn't help matters now. "I hope it's all right with you, my going after Angel, that is."

"Certainly," Garrett said and Maggie nodded her assurance.

"She's in Santa Fe," Gavin offered. "I'm leaving this afternoon."

"I don't envy you going after a willful young woman," Garret said with a sly glance cast at his wife. "Retrieving spiteful, head-strong girls, especially ones you fancy yourself in love with and plan to marry, is no easy task."

Gavin looked quizzically from his father's amused expression to his mother's reddening face. "You look as if you have a story to tell," Gavin said with a grin.

"You might say," Garrett began, "that I started a family tradition."

"You might say," Maggie interrupted, "that unless you want to sleep with that horse of yours, that you'll choose your words carefully."

Garrett grabbed her around the waist and pulled her close. "You know that your Grandfather Intissar, Maggie's pa, and I were good friends long before your mother came here to live."

Gavin nodded. "Mom lived in Kansas with her grandmother because Grandfather Intissar had some problems to work through."

"That's right and when those problems were worked out, he sent for Maggie. Only problem was, she didn't want to come. That's when I came into the picture. Jason Intissar sent for me and knowing that I was half love-sick for his daughter, he put me on a train to Topeka and paid me to fetch his only child home."

"I guess I knew that," Gavin said as if suddenly remembering the story.

Maggie interrupted his thoughts. "What your father might be hesitant to say is that I nearly outfoxed him several times, in escaping to return to my grandmother."

Garrett laughed. "She thinks she nearly outfoxed me. First I caught her coming down a trellis outside her second story bedroom window. Then she nearly got herself killed when she slipped off the train in the middle of the night and wandered around on the rain-drenched prairie for several days." His voice grew quite sober. "When you find her, Gavin," he stated quite seriously, "don't let her out of your sight. Women get peculiar notions when they feel caged in and I wouldn't want Angeline to get hurt."

Maggie had thought to make a snide remark, but the truth was, Garrett's words were an accurate portrayal of why she'd run away from him. Now Gavin would perhaps face the same thing with Angeline. Maggie put a hand on her son's arm. "Unfortunately," she said softly, "your father is right. Angeline won't be easy to bring home and it might risk the both of you before the matter is settled."

"Don't worry," Gavin said, patting his mother's hand, "God's my partner on this one, as with everything else. I prayed long and hard about Angeline and this time won't be any exception. You keep me in your prayers, too. That way, when I'm having to concentrate on what she's doing and where, I'll still be covered."

"You'll have our prayers, son," Garrett replied proudly.

"And I know you'll have Lillie and Dan's," Maggie added.

"Thanks," Gavin said and turned to leave. "I know it will make all the difference."

seven

ngeline had already been told more than ten times by Willa
at tonight's rally was an important one. She had been in-
ucted to send messages to all of her family's good friends
d encourage them to attend. After that, Willa had suggested
at Angeline rest up, and with special emphasis she added
at Angeline should wear something pretty to the rally.

Pacing in her hotel room as twilight fell in a golden glow
ainst the adobe churches and plaza structures, Angeline
cked up one of Willa's books and read for several minutes.
om outside her window came the sound of a baby crying
d for some reason it caused Angeline to think of home.

Going to the window, Angeline gazed out on the ancient
ty of Santa Fe. "I wonder if they hate me?" she whispered.
e couldn't help but envision her father and mother sitting
wn to the empty dining table and gazing at her vacated spot
e way they had when John and James had gone into the army.

"I don't know what to do," she moaned and wished that
od would open her eyes miraculously. She'd gone to church
ce she was a little girl, but none of that or the multiple
rmons and Bible verses that had made their ways to ears,
emed to help now.

Down in the center of the plaza, Angeline could see the
akings of a crowd starting to gather. Willa had told her that
any of the local politicians were shy about their cause, but
at with a little encouragement from solid citizens and people
ch as Angeline, they would turn out in mass number. If for

no other reason, just to see what the fuss was all about. As they were lucky however, as Willa told Angeline they mu be, these men would offer their support for the suffrage move ment.

Angeline felt torn like never before. She really did want t help Willa. More than that, she wanted to do something wort while with her life. Something that people would remembe her fondly for. Women's suffrage seemed to be a worth enough cause, but Angeline knew her heart wasn't in it com pletely. How could it be with part of her heart was severa hundred miles away in Bandelero?

The knock on her door startled Angeline, because she knew Willa would simply enter with her own key.

"Who is it?" she asked softly.

"Douglas."

Angeline opened the door. "Mr. Baker."

Douglas smiled revealing his perfect teeth and Angelin immediately thought of a tooth powder advertisement she' recently seen in one of her magazines.

"I hoped to escort you to the rally tonight. Willa wi undoubtably have her hands full and I wouldn't want you t arrive alone."

"That's very considerate of you, Mr. Baker."

"I thought we dispensed with that earlier today. Call m Douglas."

Angeline nodded and offered him a shy smile. "Very wel Douglas. I shall meet you in the lobby at seven o'clock."

"I will look forward to it." He gave her a slight bow an left without another word.

Angeline closed the door behind her and leaned against heavily. Every time Douglas was near her, she couldn't he but think of Gavin. The troubling part was that she couldn r the life of her figure out why.

※

n minutes 'til seven, Angeline put on the finishing touches adding a pink ribbon to her carefully pinned up hair. She anted to make Willa proud and so she had chosen her very licate white eyelet dress with the pink ribbon waist band d snug bodice. Checking herself in the mirror one final time, ngeline opened the door and made her way to the lobby.

Douglas was waiting for her at the bottom of the stairs. He st an admiring glance at her, quickly running his gaze up d down the full length of her.

"You look ravishing, my dear." His tone was sincere enough, t something in his expression seemed almost leering.

'Thank you," Angeline murmured, uncertain why she sud-nly felt so uncomfortable.

"Come along," Douglas commanded, taking hold of her n. "They are about to begin and Willa has instructed me to ve you close to the stage."

"Why would Willa want me there?"

"I'm uncertain as to her exact reasons," Douglas stated, king his way with Angeline into the street, "but I believe e holds you in high esteem. You will offer her great sup-rt as you have all along."

Angeline said nothing, but immediately began to pick up the atmosphere surrounding the plaza grounds. Somewhere the midst of the people, a band was playing popular rag-e tunes and most of the people seemed in high spirits. The wd was growing by the minute and though most of the ticipants were men, Angeline counted a great many women ong the group as well. It should please Willa, Angeline ught.

Douglas manuevered them expertly through the mass and

finally arrived at the place where Willa, in a stiff looking s
of blue serge and a banner proclaiming her cause, awai
the moment of her speech.

"Good, you're here," she said, noting Douglas' possessi
control of Angeline's movements. "Sit here and I will st
the rally."

Angeline allowed Douglas to lead her to the chair, wh
Willa had the small band stop playing their ragtime tunes a
cued the percussionist to give her a drumroll.

"Ladies and gentlemen, we are happy to welcome you h
tonight." The crowd seemed to still and move in closer to
stage. Willa began to speak in earnest, commandi
everyone's attention and enrapturing Angeline as she had
very first night in Denver.

"For centuries woman have played a vital and necessa
role in the lives of their families. When God first created
universe and mankind, He showed the necessity for woma
hood and by special design created her for life on this eart

Angeline smiled. Willa said she always liked to start w
something about God, because who could argue with
Bible? True to form, she was leading the crowd where
wanted them to go.

Willa continued, "The position women have maintained o
the last several hundred years, however, has been less o
helpmate to her male counterparts and more of a servant
servant whose mind has been closed to the reality of what
was created to do. Women all across this great nation,
even throughout the world, have offered important progr
in the lives of all people. They must be rescued from obs
rity and thrust forward in the limelight." Willa paused to
how the crowd was effected by her stern words before m
ing on.

Madame Marie Curie in 1911 won the Nobel Prize for
mistry. Her contributions to the field of science have been
gnificent and will continue to be so. And only a few years
, an upstanding southern woman named Juliette Low cre-
d an organization for our young woman—the Girl Scouts.
s association promises to help girls everywhere to formu-
 leadership qualities and push forward into the future.
wever," Willa paused and everyone seemed to lean for-
d, "that future cannot be mastered, and those young women
not be sufficiently utilized until they are able to exercise
ir choices for the leadership in this country. Women need
right to vote. Men need for women to have that right."

he crowd murmured unintelligible things, while Angeline
med to momentarily forget Willa and concentrated instead
the people nearest her. She hated to eavesdrop but she
ited to know, no, she needed to know what they were think-
Douglas seemed to immediately sense her contemplation
leaned down to whisper in her ear.

Smart men will know she speaks the truth and if their
nen are motivated to seek the vote, they will rally behind
n."

ngeline looked up at Douglas for a moment and nodded,
le Willa finished her speech and prepared to move from
stage to walk amidst her listeners and answer questions.
or some strange reason Angeline suddenly felt very mis-
:ed. She felt the people around her shifting to accommo-
 those in front of them and a fearfulness gripped her mo-
itarily. With a quick glance at Douglas, Angeline assured
self that all was well.

/illa shook hands with people, while Douglas helped
geline to her feet. "She's very good at this," Douglas said
"sensing Angeline's uneasiness. "Just watch her and you

will learn a great deal."

Suddenly, a man approached Willa with an narrowing
his eyes that quickly told Angeline he wasn't a supporter
the "cause."

"Madam," the man began in a loud enough voice that e
eryone around immediately fell silent. "I have listened to y
suffragettes from one end of this country to the other. Y
spout about rights that were never extended to you, becau
frankly, madam, they were never necessary. Proper wome
women who are biblical minded as you so clearly like to
sociate your cause to, seek the protection and authority
men. Men, whom I might add, the good Lord made first a
put in charge of everything else." At this, a roar of appro
went up from the crowd.

"Sir, proper women are women who seek to do their be
They are women who, knowing God gave them many gi
chose not to waste a single one. They seek not to usurp
authority of man, but to augment the benefits they might of
their fellow human beings."

The man made several notes on a tablet before question
Willa again. This time the attack was far more personal a
an ugliness was born of the group that startled Angeline.

"Why is it, madam, that all of you suffragettes are home
spinster-type women, who obviously can't seem to attract
attention of a man any other way, than to try to steal the pa
from him?" The people surrounding them roared in laugh
and Angeline moved closer to Douglas, feeling fearful t
things might get physical as Willa had warned her had h
pened on occasion.

Without any warning, Willa seemed to part the crowd v
the wave of her hand and pulled Angeline forward. "T
lovely young woman is my assistant. Perhaps you would

ll her how homely and spinster-like she is."

he man stared at the stunned-faced Angeline and smiled.
, madam," he said to Willa and a broad smile crossed his
. "I doubt anyone could accuse this beauty of being
ely."

ngeline wanted to crawl into the nearest hole, but Willa's
d firmly gripped her arm and moving away was out of the
tion. The man quickly motioned to someone and Angeline
ked her surprise when a man thrust a camera into her face
started snapping pictures. The flash blinded her momen-
y, but Angeline stood fast.

ell me, miss," the man began.

Her name is Angeline Monroe. She is the very model of
e and grace," Willa stated for the newspaperman.

ell me, Miss Monroe," he began again with pencil in
l, "do you honestly support the cause of suffrage and if
vhy?"

ngeline felt Willa's hand tighten on her arm, but she wasn't
oled enough to know this was her mentor's signal to re-
n silent. Willa opened her mouth the speak, but found
eline's soft voice answering instead.

hold the highest regard for womanhood. I believe that
has given women a very special place on this earth and
place is neither to usurp the man's place, nor to exceed
The crowd grew completely silent as everyone strained to
the delicate voice.

My own mother is an intelligent woman who works at the
of my father, a physician. She is often consulted for her
ion and my father, even with his college training, sup-
s and honors my mother as a colleague. Other women I
w are just as resourceful and just as important. And sir, I
it sad indeed that you seem to place a woman's value

only in her appearance. One cannot always help the way
looks. Should we scorn the cripple because he," Ange
paused, "or she, cannot walk as we do with strong, st
legs? Do we not love the unlovable, just as Christ did w
He walked this earth?"

The man stopped writing and stared at Angeline in earr
Several women in the crowd dabbed at their eyes with ha
kerchiefs, while their men stared down at their feet and shi
uncomfortably.

"The Lord made us all," Angeline continued. "Who are
to condemn that which He created? You, sir, report the n
with the critical eye of one who has seen many things
perhaps has seen too much. You have lost in your sens
vision what it is to feel the heartfelt sorrow of the pe
around you. We are not seeking to thrust you from your pl
We are merely asking to join you there. We are asking yo
be proud of your women, your wives, mothers, sisters,
daughters. If we lack wisdom and education, then teach
If we lack courage, then bolster us with your own, but d
turn us away as though you were ashamed. Not a single
here can boast of an entry into this world without the a
tance of a woman. We are now asking for the return of
favor in assisting us into the world. We are asking fo
right to vote."

For several minutes no one said anything. There were
fling sounds that were heard and then the sound of a sol
pair of hands clapping, then two, then a dozen, then a
dred. Willa smiled to herself, smug in the realization
Angeline had won over the crowd and shamed them into
port. She gave her protegee a hearty pat on the back be
nodding to Douglas. Angeline Monroe would be a bigge
set than even Willa Neal had imagined.

eight

It was as though that one small speech had somehow justified Angeline's existence in Willa Neal's eyes. She beheld the girl with a new respect and the fervent, driving knowledge that Angeline just might get them voting rights in New Mexico.

The papers that ran the following morning were plastered with front page photographs of Angeline Monroe. Her speech was recited, almost word for word, and the article citing it listed Angeline as a remarkable and clear-minded suffragette.

Willa was thrilled at the coverage. They often had to pay out precious money to get the kind of newspaper attention that Angeline's one, heart-felt outburst had surged. She poured over the stories and the multiple requests which had started arriving as early as six that morning, for interviews with Angeline Monroe.

Further evidence came in the form of flowers and cards from the political connections whom Angeline had invited to the speech. Willa read one card after another, noting the dates and times of invitations to dinners, small parties and teas. She intended to work the situation to her benefit no matter the consumption of Angeline's time and energies.

The one bit of attention that Willa would not tolerate came from the more conservative suffragists who sought to have Angeline join their cause instead of Willa's more militant one. Willa refused to even admit these women into the hotel suite and Angeline couldn't help but wonder what the real threat might be. Willa passed it off as unimportant, however, and insisted Angeline read a speech that had been given by Alice Paul several years earlier and not concern herself with the merits of the less passionate.

Angeline, herself, loved the attention. Used to the lime light, she was once again thrust front and center and it was everything she'd hoped it would be. A surprising sideline came to her in the form of Douglas' ardent regard.

Angeline enjoyed Douglas' pampering, but her heart nagged at her and reminded her that Gavin was at home in Bandelero waiting for her. *But I never committed myself to him*, Angeline thought. *In fact, I told him that I wasn't interested in marriage.* She reminded herself of this at least twenty times a day, for all the good it did.

When Willa announced they were moving on to the next city, Angeline was a bit taken back. She hadn't thought of how far she was drifting from home and the people she loved until Willa pointed out that they would be traveling for sev eral weeks. Guilty at the thought of her parent's suffering because of her disappearance, Angeline suggested to Willa that she write or telegraph them, but Willa quickly dismissed the idea.

"They won't understand and they'll only insist that you come home," Willa replied. Angeline nodded in acquiescence, but felt a terrible lump in her throat at the thought of her parents worrying over her.

&

Two days later, Angeline found herself sitting to the far side of the stage, where Willa, front and center, urged the people of the small town to see the merits of women's suffrage. This town was much smaller than Santa Fe and far less progres sive in its thinking. Many of the men and women gathered there were natives to the area and cared little for the ideals behind voting when they were worried about water for their crops and animals.

Angeline was amazed at the crowd's seeming indifference, but even more amazing was the way that this indifference changed to anger at one simple statement made by Willa.

"I have seen the treatment of animals in this country and deemed it better than that of women," she announced in a heated fury.

"Animals are our life's blood," a man yelled from the murmuring crowd.

Willa shook her raised fist and Angeline felt herself cower against the hard wooden chair. She didn't much care for this side of Willa. "Women gave you life, not those animals you pamper to market."

This created quite a stir in the gathering and before Angeline realized what was happening there were angry shouts and rocks being thrown at Willa.

Staring in dumbstruck silence, Angeline watched as several men approached the stage. They were shouting and cursing about Willa's inability to understand their plight. It wouldn't be learned until days later that several boxcars filled with sheep headed to market had derailed and consequently pushed more than one of the local families into financial ruin.

Angeline came to her feet at the sight of the first dissenter coming on stage. She backed up against the edge, not knowing what would happen next, fearful that she would be unable to protect herself from the rushing crowd.

Glancing around into the inky shadows of full night, Angeline began to pray as never before. "Please God," she whispered, "please help me."

Utter pandemonium broke out after that and the stage was

rushed with Willa being safely spirited off in the opposite direction of where Angeline stood. Without warning, Angeline felt herself being lifted and thrown heavily against the broad shoulders of a stranger. She fought for all she was worth, kicking, screaming, and beating at the man's back, but nothing could stop him.

The man pushed through the crowds, leaving the dissenters behind to tear up the stage and suffrage banners. He wormed his way through new arrivals who were clearly endowed with false courage from the assistance of the local saloon. When her captor started to run, Angeline felt the wind knock from her as her mid-section slammed against his shoulder again and again.

"Dear God," she breathed aloud, feeling herself grow faint.

Then as quickly as it had begun, it ended. The man stopped, glanced around, and opened the small wooden door that entered a tiny adobe building.

He had to stoop to get through the doorway, but once inside he straightened back up and pulled Angeline down into his arms.

Angeline kept her eyes closed tightly. Partially because she was afraid to see her captor and partially because her head was spinning.

"Hi, Angel," the stern, but familiar voice called out, as Gavin Lucas cradled her to his chest.

Angeline's eyes flew open and a small gasp escaped her lips before she threw her arms around Gavin's neck and squealed his name.

"Gavin! I'm so happy to see you. I thought I was going to die back there!"

"You very well could have. Those people weren't a bit happy with your cause." He said the word in such a snide way that Angeline immediately took offense.

"They just don't understand," she began. "They don't see the necessity of women being allowed to choose their representation in government." She wound down a bit and looked around the room. "Where are we?"

"I haven't the slightest idea," Gavin replied. "I looked in the window and saw the place was empty and figured I needed to check you out and see if you were all right. Are you?" His expression was one of sober consideration, while his eyes traveled the length of Angeline's simple white shirtwaist and blue serge skirt.

Angeline noted that her suffrage ribbon had somehow been torn from her and was probably beneath the muddy boots of the town's male population. Otherwise, she felt fine now that she could breathe. "I'm perfectly well," she finally answered.

"Good." Gavin's voice still sounded rather indifferent. "We'd better get out of here and get back to the hotel."

"You're staying at the hotel?" Angeline questioned. "Why are you here, Gavin?" she pressed without giving him a chance to answer her first question.

Gavin opened the door and peered down the alleyway in each direction. He motioned her to the door with his finger pressed to his lips to insure her silence.

Angeline was never good at keeping quiet, however. Especially when she wanted answers to important questions. She stared up at the handsome face of the man who claimed to love her and whispered, "Why?"

Gavin looked down at her as though she'd asked the stupidest question possible. "Why do you think?" he replied softly and pulled her into the shrouding darkness.

Angeline didn't like leaving the lighted room, but she liked the idea of awaiting the return of an angry owner even less.

She allowed Gavin to pull her along until they approached the main street and saw that at least twenty or thirty angry men still surrounded the front doors to the hotel.

"Come on," Gavin growled in a barely audible voice. He pushed Angeline toward the end of the boardwalk and ended up pulling her into the livery at the edge of town before he'd allow her to rest.

"What in the world is wrong with you, Gavin Lucas?"

"Me? You think there's something wrong with me?" His voice was indignant.

"Yes," Angeline began, but Gavin wouldn't hear any more.

"I came here because your mother and father are sick with worry and grief about your well-being. I've followed you from Santa Fe and tried a hundred times to get close enough to talk to you, but you have more watchdogs than prime herd of beef on its way to market." Angeline started to respond to his reference, but closed her mouth quickly at the look of warning Gavin gave her.

"I nearly get killed in that crowd, just to save your scrawny, ungrateful neck, and you have the audacity to ask me why I came here?"

Angeline was quite taken back at this side of Gavin. She knew him to be quite serious and decidedly dedicated to his loved ones, but she'd never seen him this mad. "I'm. . . I'm . . ." she wanted the words to be just right, but they wouldn't come together.

"You're what?" Gavin asked her as if he thought her reply might actually be important.

"I'm sorry." Angeline finally managed to say. "I never meant to hurt my folks, but the cause is important."

"You and your causes!" Gavin exclaimed in disgust. "Your cause got a little out of hand tonight, don't you think?"

"I didn't expect it to result in a fight," Angeline admitted, taking a seat on a nearby bale of straw.

Just then the livery keeper entered from outside. "Oh!" he exclaimed. "I didn't know I had company. Sorry to keep you waiting, but it seems we had a bit of excitement at the hotel tonight."

"No problem," Gavin replied and nodded, toward Angeline. "I had a bit of excitement tonight, myself."

The man looked at Angeline, nodded and gave Gavin a sly wink. "I'll be out back if you need me, but I suppose you won't." Then the man left as though it were perfectly normal to find two strangers arguing in his livery.

Angeline jerked herself upright and glared at Gavin. "I'll not have you besmirch my reputation by implying that you and I, that we, that we. . . ." she blushed furiously and fell silent.

"That we what? That we raced through the streets, fighting to save our own necks?"

Angeline stomped her foot, unable to unleash enough words at once to tell Gavin Lucas just what she thought of him. "Go home, Gavin," she finally uttered and turned to walk toward the door.

Gavin spun her around and pulled her into his arms. "They're using you, Angel. I've heard the way they talk behind your back. I've been following them, remember? They just want to use you until you can't help them any more."

Angeline pushed against Gavin and to her surprise he released her. "Mind your own business, Gavin."

"You are my business, Angel," he replied softly. "I intend to marry you or did you forget that?"

Angeline tried to sound self-confident when she laughed. "It's immaterial what you intend. The cause needs me and I intend to fight for women's suffrage in any way I can. It's a cause worth fighting for."

"Is it a cause worth dying for?"

Gavin's words seem to hit some deeply buried reality in Angeline, but she hated to yield that conquest to him. "I'm not sure any cause is worth dying for," she replied honestly. "At least, I'm not sure I've found a cause worth that to me."

Gavin stepped forward and reached out to her. When Angeline didn't refuse his touch, Gavin pulled her close. "What about God, Angel. Where does God fit into your cause?"

"Why do you ask that?" Angeline whispered, staring deep into Gavin's smoky blue eyes.

"You were sure calling on Him for help a little while ago. I was just wondering how He figures into your plans for the future. Or does He have a place in your plans?"

The spell was broken and once again Angeline pushed away and headed for the door. "He has a much more secure position than you do, Mr. Lucas." The words were delivered with stilted exasperation. Lifting her chin defiantly, Angeline continued, "Now if you don't mind, I intend to return to my hotel room. I'm quite exhausted."

nine

Gavin left Angeline at the door to her hotel room and went downstairs to make plans for going back to Bandelero. He figured he had more than enough money to get them home, but he had no idea of how he was going to convince Angel to go, short of hog-tying her and throwing her over his shoulder. Laughing to himself, Gavin thought even that plan had its merits.

Inside her room, Angeline tiptoed to avoid disturbing Willa, but the woman had incredible hearing and quickly came to investigate.

"Angeline! Where have you been, I was worried that you'd been hurt in the unrest."

"Unrest? Is that what you call that riot of out-of-control rock slingers?" Angeline shook her head. "I've never seen people like that, Willa. There was no reasoning with them at all."

Willa's brown hair hung in a loose braid down her back and when she smiled at Angeline's statement, she was almost attractive. Angeline couldn't help but think that with just a little make-up and the right clothes, Willa could actually be beautiful.

"You're smiling at me," Angeline sighed in exasperation. "You were nearly killed and you're smiling?"

"I'm smiling because this entire ordeal was mild compared to what we saw in Washington D.C. in years past. Angeline, you are young and innocent. It is hard for you to realize that things worth fighting for often come at a high price." Willa paused and looked around the room. "Did you read those speeches I gave you? The ones given by Alice Paul and Lucy Burns?" Angeline nodded with a shudder. Willa smiled patiently. "It wasn't a pretty picture that they painted about the treatment of suffragettes in England, was it?"

"No, it wasn't," Angeline recalled. "I found it deplorable that one human being could treat another in such a fashion."

Willa looked thoughtful for a moment. "Those women believed in the cause of suffrage so strongly that they starved themselves in massive hunger strikes. The public was enraged, shocked, surprised, and concerned. The feelings ran from the extremes of wanting to put these women in insane asylums to the sympathetic desires of those who understood their plight."

"But they forced them to eat," Angeline said with disgust, then shook her head. "No, it couldn't be called eating. They ran tubes down their throats to their stomachs. I could never have imagined such actions possible."

"They are, and even worse things than these have been endured by our sister suffragettes."

Angeline put her hand to her head. The entire evening had been too much for her. "I need to go to bed."

Willa watched her carefully for a moment. "How did you escape the crowd? Did Douglas find you?"

"No, I never saw Douglas. A friend of the family, someone my parents sent to find me, did just that and rescued me as the stage was overrun."

Willa frowned at this news, glad that Angeline had already turned to walk towards her door. "A friend? Did he sympathize with the cause?"

Angeline laughed. "No, Gavin Lucas only sympathizes with

is own causes. The main one of which seems to be his de-
ire to marry me." Without another word to consider the
ituation, she left Willa.

Willa stared at the closed door of Angeline's room for sev-
ral minutes before quickly going to her own room to dress.
he had to get to Douglas and see what could be done to
iscourage this Gavin Lucas character. She couldn't lose
ngeline now. Not when there was so much at stake.

Forty-five minutes later, Douglas Baker finished counting
ut several dollars to each of three scruffy looking charac-
rs. Men could be bought easily in the small town and get-
ng what he needed had been no trouble at all.

"You understand," Douglas stated before turning to leave,
I don't want him killed. I just want him too busy with his
wn problems to stick his nose in ours." The men nodded
nd watched the well-dressed man disappear down the alley
ay. Looking at each other and sensing that the time to earn
eir ill-gotten pay was at hand, the men took off in the oppo-
te direction.

⁓

But I don't understand," Angeline protested, taking her seat
n the train. "Why are we running away and to Denver of all
laces?"

"We aren't running away, so much as tactically regroup-
g," Douglas said with an air of concern. "We have to con-
olidate our forces, much like an army. We need to approach
ese small towns with proof of the benefits that can be had
rough acceptance of suffrage." Douglas seemed unruffled
y the entire episode, while Angeline had slept very little the
ight before. The dark circles under her eyes betrayed her
xhaustion and Douglas reached out his hand. "Come sit be-
de me," he spoke softly. "You may use my shoulder for a

pillow."

Angeline was touched by his kind gesture, but shook her head. "I'm afraid that would hardly be proper, Douglas."

"But we are friends and in clear view of everyone on board. Come, Angeline." His words lured her into obedience. "No one will think a thing of it."

"Maybe for just a short time," she whispered, feeling incapable of refusing.

While Angeline slept she dreamed of Gavin. It had been with a bit of sadness and relief that she had been unable to see him before leaving town with Willa and Douglas. Had her words and declaration of independence put him off so that he left without her? Perhaps he was too busy elsewhere to concern himself with Angeline's needs. Needs? Angeline wondered even in her sleep what those needs might be. Restless from her thoughts, she turned away from Douglas' rather soft shoulder and sought the hard, cool glass of the window beside her.

After two days on the train, Angeline was grateful to be in Denver. She loved Denver with it's big buildings and bustling streets. She liked the automobiles and smartly dressed people who always seemed to be hurrying to some place important.

She was immediately whisked away to one of Denver' finer hotels and given a suite to herself, much to her surprise. Willa suggested she bathe and sleep, something that Angeline surmised Willa longed for herself.

Angeline looked the room over casually. It was very nice, in fact, it was the nicest hotel she had ever stayed in. There was a small sitting room with a door leading off to a private bath and another door leading to a bedroom. The sitting room was tastefully furnished with several velvet upholstered chairs

d a round table of walnut that held a crystal vase of freshly
t flowers. The plush draperies had been pulled back to real a charming view of the city, with a small park across the
eet in which Angeline hoped to find time to walk.

"I can't say that I haven't been well cared for," Angeline
urmured and went to prepare her bath. In the back of her
ind, however, she once again let her thoughts travel back to
avin.

"I wonder why he didn't come to tell me goodbye?" Then
soon as the words were out of her mouth, Angeline real-
ed there was no way Gavin could have known of her plans.
ngeline herself hadn't known they were leaving until Willa
d her dressed and on the train.

Soaking in the tub of hot water, Angeline let down her long
ond hair. She eased down into the tub, sighing at the sooth-
g comfort it offered. *With very little trouble,* she thought, *I
uld fall asleep here.* But, knowing the bed would be more
nducive to her needs, Angeline forced herself to finish the
sk at hand.

&

hen the loud knock sounded on her hotel room door,
ngeline forced herself to wake up. She glanced quickly
ound her, forgetting momentarily where she was. Another
rce knock, followed by the sound of a key being fitted in
e door, caused Angeline to jerk up in the bed.

"Angeline!" It was Willa.

"In here," she called out and forced herself to leave the
mfort of the bed.

Willa bounded in with all the energy of six women and
iled. "We've got a great deal of work to do. I've ordered
pper to be sent here so get dressed and join me."

Angeline nodded and reached for her blue serge suit. It

was one of only four outfits she had and she was rapidly be
ginning to tire from her limited wardrobe. With a sigh
Angeline couldn't help but remember the closet filled with
clothes at home in Bandelero.

By the time Angeline had dressed and repinned her hair
supper had arrived and with it a very pleasant aroma.

"Ummm, that smells heavenly," Angeline voiced, coming
to join Willa.

"This hotel offers the finest meals," Willa said motioning
Angeline to sit. "Of course you'll soon find that out for your
self."

Angeline looked down at the steaming food and realized
had been a long time since she'd eaten. Happily, she joined
Willa, offered a small prayer of thanks, and sliced into the
most tender veal cutlet ever created.

"Douglas and I both realize that this constant moving about
is taxing to you, but you are young and can adapt easily."
Willa took a bite of food and chewed thoughtfully as though
carefully considering what she was about to say. "I need for
you to understand, Angeline, that often you will have no say
in what happens and you may have questions. I hope that you
will have the wisdom to not question me in public, but when
we are alone you may of course seek me out."

"What are we going to do next?" Angeline jumped right i

"Well," Willa said, "we have a great deal of planning. We
have the march on Washington coming up and we must some
how rally our sisters there to aid the cause of winning New
York. They will put the suffrage issue to a vote this Novem
ber and we must take that state or it will notably hinder o
cause."

"Why is that?" Angeline asked innocently.

"Because Washington can only be swayed by powerf

eople. It matters little what the common man wants, if the
alms of those in control are being tied to the purse strings of
e rich. New York is filled with persuasive people. Rich,
mous people who can see the thing done," Willa stated
lmost feverishly. "We must win in New York and to do so,
e must make a good showing in Washington."

Angeline listened while Willa continued, but her heart was
lsewhere and far from the cause of suffrage. Something
aused her to remember the warm way Gavin's arms had held
er and from that moment on, Angeline heard nothing that
Villa said.

"You aren't even listening to me."

"I'm sorry, Willa. My mind and heart are heavy."

"The young man in New Mexico?" Willa questioned with-
ut sympathy.

"Yes." Angeline sighed and hoped Willa could relate to
er feelings. She could not.

"You cannot trust this person, Angeline!" Willa was quite
damant in her statement. "Men are corrupt. Why even Dou-
las is only trusted so far."

Angeline's head snapped up. "I don't believe you can just
m up an entire group of people like that, Willa. Isn't that
hat men are trying to do to us?"

"It's different." Willa seemed to have to think on the mat-
r for a moment. "It's an entirely different matter."

"How?" Angeline questioned. "Men state that women
houldn't be allowed to vote because we are poorly educated
nd easily swayed. Now you're telling me that men as a whole
e corrupt and incapable of receiving our trust. How is it
ifferent?"

Willa got to her feet as if deeply hurt. "I can see this con-
ersation will get us no where. You are naive and young,

Angeline, and you need to trust my wisdom on the matter. [I] will leave you to yourself. See if you can't sort through you[r] childishness." With that Willa left the room, slamming th[e] door behind her.

Angeline stared in surprise for several moments before go[o]ing to the door and locking it. "Whatever got into her[?]" Angeline wondered aloud. It never crossed her mind to re[c]ognize Willa's confusion in how to control Angeline.

"Well, what am I to do now?"

Crossing the room to look out on the darkness that had ca[p]tured the city, Angeline spied a black-covered book on a sma[ll] table by the window. A Bible. Angeline recognized it imme[e]diately. Almost against her will, she picked up the book an[d] held it close. All of her life she had been taught to cent[er] herself around the teachings here. All of her life she'd bee[n] told to make her stand on this book alone.

Taking a seat, Angeline opened the Bible and flipped cas[u]ally through the pages until she came to rest on 2 Timoth[y] chapter three, verses thirteen through fifteen. "But evil me[n] and seducers shall wax worse and worse, deceiving, and b[e]ing deceived. But continue thou in the things which thou ha[st] learned and hast been assured of, knowing of whom thou ha[st] learned them; And that from a child thou hast known the ho[ly] scriptures, which are able to make thee wise unto salvati[on] through faith which is in Christ Jesus."

The words were a powerful message to Angeline and s[he] read them over many times before leaning back in the cha[ir] to close the Bible. "I've known since I was a small child th[at] the truth of God could be found in scripture," she murmure[d]. "I know the answers must be here, but I'm so confused. [I] care for Gavin and I know he cares for me, but the cause [is] also important and Willa is right about the corruption of m[en] nd powerful people."

With a sigh, Angeline shook her head and put the Bible side. There didn't seem to be a clear understanding. At least ot one that came easily.

ten

The next week and a half passed in a flurry of activities fo
Angeline. She met many of Willa's more militant suffrag
supporters and found these women to be even more intoleran
of opposition, than Willa was. Angeline listened graciousl
as each woman recited her entry into the "cause" and tried t
be sympathetic or enraged at exactly the precise moment fo
each, depending on the subject on which the woman spoke.

Angeline then found herself in a grown-up school of sorts
She was given printings of lectures, handwritten copies o
letters, as well as lists of statistics regarding suffrage world
wide. Next, she was lectured morning, noon, and night unt
she no longer questioned why she was asked to respond in
certain way, she simply did it. Which, of course, was exactl
as Willa Neal planned it.

After an intensive period of this oppressive training
Angeline found herself at a reception the Governor was throw
ing. People from assorted causes gathered at this party wit
the hopes and planned intentions of gaining the ear of th
powerful. And, while suffrage had already been achieved i
Colorado, there was a great deal the suffragettes hoped t
obtain from their political representatives.

Angeline passed through the beautifully decorated ball roor
and spoke with a number of people. Some she knew vaguel
and others quite well, and to whomever she spoke, she spok
of suffrage.

"Angeline Monroe?" the voice of an elderly gentlema

sounded behind her.

Angeline whirled around, surprised that the man seemed to know her, while she hadn't the faintest clue as to who he was.

"You don't remember me and in truth, had I not overheard someone speak of you a moment ago, I wouldn't have recognized you from the scrappy ten-year-old I met long ago."

"I'm afraid you have me at a disadvantage," Angeline replied with a smile.

"Jefferson Ashton," the man replied and extended his hand. "I'm a good friend of your father's. He was a great ally in the fight to win statehood in 1912."

Angeline remained confused, struggling to put his face with the newly given name. "My father has many friends, Mr. Ashton. Forgive me if I don't remember you."

The man chuckled. "There's naught to forgive, my dear. You were just a child. Your father first met me when I sought him on a medical emergency. One of my entourage became quite ill from bad oysters. Your father saved his life and in the process he and I discussed the volatile politics of the day. Now I find you here in Colorado and at a political gathering no less. Tell me, what is it that you are about these days?"

"I'm in support of suffrage," Angeline told the gray-haired man. She liked his kindly face and long droopy mustache. He had a glint in his eyes that bespoke of a brain that never stopped working. "I'm here with Willa Neal."

"Ahh," the man said as though the mere name of Willa Neal said it all. "Then you are in agreement with the more militant champions of suffrage."

Angeline smiled thoughtfully at Mr. Ashton. "I don't always believe they go about things in the proper manner. I'm not sure that I would go on hunger strikes and storm the President's house with threats of forming a separate country for women."

Ashton laughed at this. "I've heard of the extremist also. say give them a country somewhere, as long as it's not here."

"I suppose that would get them out of your hair." Angeline enjoyed the older man's sense of humor.

"In truth, those women do far more to harm the cause than to help it. When Colorado first accepted suffrage many other states were interested and encouraged. Now many, many year later, we still haven't seen nationwide suffrage come to pas and I believe it is because of the frightening antics of the more dramatic of your sisters."

Angeline's lavender eyes narrowed a bit as she considered his words. "I have often wondered if having the vote merited civil disobedience. It seemed to me that children do not often get their way with tantrums as much as with cooperative be havior. The same seemed to be a natural assumption for na tional causes."

"Right you are, my dear." Jefferson Ashton accepted drink from a passing waiter. "You are very wise, Miss Mon roe and, I believe, cool-headed like your father."

Angeline smiled. "Yes, I rarely get angry. But, as my mothe would say, when I do, watch out!"

"So what will you do now, Miss Monroe?"

"It is Miss Neal's desire that I accompany them to Wash ington and join in the rally there. We are to speak with th President and request more support for a nationwide push fc suffrage."

"My advice to you, regarding Woodrow," Mr. Ashton re marked, noting his close friendship with the President, "is t be clear-minded and open to suggestion. He is a fair mar but he has a great deal on his mind these days. Things that f outweigh the necessity of suffrage."

"But suffrage is very important!" Angeline exclaimed. "Some of these women are dying for the cause."

"And some of our young men may be called upon to die for another." Jefferson Ashton's words hit Angeline hard.

"The war in Europe," she murmured.

"Yes. It isn't likely that we can remain neutral much longer."

"My brothers both joined the army," Angeline said with a fretful look on her face. "I pray you are wrong."

Mr. Ashton offered her a sympathetic look and gently touched her arm. "I pray also that I am." He tried to be consoling while giving her the honesty that she desired. "Wars are ugly things, Miss Monroe, and I have no desire for us to enter into this particular mess without the deepest of regard."

"We shouldn't have to go at all," Angeline said rather hostilely. "Neither side is right."

Jefferson Ashton smiled at the naivete in Angeline's words. "My dear," he began in an almost indignant tone, "war in and of itself is never right. This issue goes beyond whether war is immoral or not, but whether one side is more right than the other. And in this case, there is evidence to clearly support the issue. Consider the *Lusitania*."

Angeline shook her head. "It may be true that the Germans sunk the *Lusitania* and violated the lives of Americans, but how very different is that from the way the British board our ships on the high seas? Ships, I might remind you, which are from a neutral country and headed for yet another neutral country."

"Ah, but how neutral are those countries?" Ashton questioned. "The export of food commodities to neutral counties surrounding Germany has greatly increased. Coincidence? I think not. The British confiscate our foods, label it contraband, and often haul our ships into port to avoid being attacked while sitting motionless on the ocean."

"Exactly my point," Angeline declared. "Where lies the difference between the British and the Germans?"

Jefferson Ashton smiled sadly. "The British injustices could be compensated to us later; for while the British seize ships, Germany is sinking them and taking the lives of innocent people with them. Do we, as responsible, God-fearing people, ignore the suffering and pain when we have it in our power to put an end to it?"

"But at what cost?" Angeline questioned. "Do I send my brothers to die for another woman's brothers?"

Mr. Ashton could see that Angeline was near to tears. "My dear," he spoke softly, "it is not for us to decide. We must pray and allow God to work His course and pray for those who make the choices for us." Angeline nodded, but she felt a heaviness in her heart that ruined the evening for her.

⋅⋅⋅

From a distance, Douglas Baker had watched the exchange between Angeline and Jefferson Ashton. When Willa passed by on her way from one group of congressmen to another, Douglas pulled her aside.

"Do you know who that is?" he questioned, motioning to Angeline and Ashton.

"Of course," Willa replied rather indignantly. "Everyone knows him."

"It would seem our little Angeline knows him quite well."

Willa watched for a moment as Angeline and Jefferson Ashton continued in deep conversation.

"Perhaps another family friend," Willa said with a smile. "I must say that this child has proven to be more beneficial than I'd originally believed."

"Yes," Douglas murmured, watching with envy at the

casual way Ashton touched Angeline's arm.

Just then, Angeline pulled away from Ashton and seemed to be making her goodbyes. She passed by Douglas, with a hint of tears in her eyes.

"Angeline, are you all right?" Douglas questioned her, sounding far more concerned than he really needed to.

"I'm fine," Angeline replied. "I think, however, I'm going to go upstairs to my room. I'm feeling rather tired and a bit hungry."

"They're serving a wonderful buffet," Willa reminded Angeline. "Why not have something to eat here?"

"I need to get away from all of these people," Angeline stated.

"Why not come with me to dinner? The hotel has excellent fare, which you already have learned, of course. We could go to the dining room and order something there. It would be both quiet and private," Douglas offered.

Willa sensed his game and encouraged Angeline to accept. "Douglas is right. Go on with him and afterwards, if you are still feeling poorly, Douglas will escort you to your room."

Angeline looked into the warm glow of Douglas' green eyes. She forgot for a moment about the threat of war and her brothers, but no matter how hard she tried, Angeline couldn't forget Gavin.

"I suppose, I could. . ." she began, but Douglas wouldn't allow her to finish.

"Come," he whispered in her ear.

≈

The atmosphere of the dining room was warm and inviting. Candles graced each table, giving off a romantic glow to the room and from the upstairs alcove, chamber music floated down upon the patrons like a soft satin coverlet.

Angeline tried to enjoy Douglas' praise for her work with the suffrage cause. She tried also to relish his admiration for her physical attributes, appreciative that he worked hard to keep from becoming too personal in his assessment of her.

Douglas spoke on, or droned on as Angeline heard it, while in her mind were images of that warm night when Gavin had rescued her from the angry crowd. She could feel Gavin's arms around her and smell his spicy cologne. Why hadn't he come to see her? Had he taken seriously her words of dismissal?

Unable to concentrate on Douglas, Angeline ate and tried to nod from time to time as though she were paying him the strictest attention.

"What will you do when suffrage is won?" Douglas questioned and Angeline snapped her head up as though she'd just been accused of taking the silver.

"What?" her voice betrayed her surprise.

"What will you do when suffrage is won? Will you return home to New Mexico or will you go on to fight another cause?"

Angeline stared at Douglas for a moment and thought of Gavin's harsh words for her causes. Yet, without giving it much thought at all, Angeline answered Douglas in a way that surprised him almost more than she surprised herself. "I suppose I'll go home and marry."

"Is there someone waiting for you?" Douglas asked, trying to make the question sound as though it were unimportant.

"Yes," Angeline replied, realizing for the first time that there really was someone waiting for her and that she was glad he was. But was he? She'd told Gavin to leave her alone. She'd insisted to him that she wanted nothing to do with marriage.

Just then, Douglas spotted an old friend and excused him-

f to corner the powerful land baron. While Angeline
tched, Douglas laughed and pounded the equally pleased
an on the back. They seemed completely engrossed with
ch other. When Douglas took an offered seat at the man's
le, Angeline felt rather put out and summoned the waiter.
"Please tell Mr. Baker, when he returns," she said, refrain-
g from using the words "if he returns," "that I have ac-
red a headache and have retired to my room." The man
omised to deliver the message and helped Angeline from
e table.

She hated to lie. She didn't have a headache, but in truth,
ngeline knew she soon would, if she had to listen to Dou-
as any longer. Making her way to her room, Angeline grew
eply troubled by her thoughts of Gavin. In a sense, she
as planning to marry him and the thought shocked her. She'd
own Gavin all of her life. He was probably her best friend
all the world. Could she jeopardize that with marriage?

Angeline wearily entered her hotel room, thankful for the
ectric lights that snapped on at her touch. She closed the
or behind her and turned to lock it.

"Evening, Angel. I wondered if you'd ever make it back."

Angeline turned around and gasped Gavin's name before
e even saw him. "What are you. . ." her words fell into
ence at the sight of Gavin's battered face. "Oh Gavin!"
e rushed to where he sat and lost her footing.

Gavin reached out and caught her, pulling her to his lap.
e effort caused him much pain, which was quickly reflected
his expression.

"What happened to you!? How did you get hurt?" Angeline
emed unconcerned that she was sitting on his lap. She ten-
rly reached up to touch his face. "Who did this?"

eleven

Gavin eyed Angeline suspiciously for a moment and th
sighed. "I wondered if you knew about it," he muttered.

"Knew about what?" Angeline questioned, her eyes roa
ing his face, itemizing his injuries.

"About the men who attacked me." Gavin's voice was v
grave and Angeline suddenly realized that he thought she h
a part in his injuries.

"Gavin Lucas!" she exclaimed and tried to get up from
lap. "How could you ever believe me capable of hurting y
I could never hurt you. I. . ." her mouth snapped shut wh
she realized that she'd very nearly told Gavin that she lov
him.

Sensing what she nearly said, Gavin gave her a lop-sid
grin. "No, I never really thought you were in on it, Ang
But it's good to know how you feel."

"Let me up," Angel demanded, blushing crimson from h
to toe.

"You sure?" Gavin asked, his smiled broadening. "I k
of like it like this."

Angeline pushed away and got to her feet. "You wou
Now tell me what happened to you. Who did this?"

Gavin winced as he shifted his weight. "I don't know
names, but I'd be able to pick at the faces, or what's lef
them."

Angeline grimaced. "How many?"

"Three," Gavin said rather proudly. "But they were p

...es." His words sounded more like an accounting of a poor ...hing day than an assault on his life.

Angeline ran a glance the full length of Gavin's body be-...re she spoke again. "Are you hurt anywhere else?"

Gavin laughed weakly. "You could say that. I've got some ...etty tender ribs and about fourteen stitches where the knife ...ent through my shoulder."

"Knife!" Angeline exclaimed and not caring how it looked, ...e went to Gavin's side and fell on her knees. Taking his ...nd she said, "I'm so sorry, Gavin. Oh, if you hadn't fol-...wed me you would never have gotten hurt."

Gavin was rather taken back by her reaction. If he'd ...ubted her innocence before, there was no longer any possi-...ity in his mind that Angeline had participated in planning ...s attack.

Gavin tightened his fingers around her hand. "It's okay, ...gel."

"No, it's not. I knew the crowds could get violent. It is, ...er all, my cause. But you had no way of knowing that people ...uld be so set against the suffrage movement. If you hadn't ...me to try and talk me into going home, you wouldn't have ...d to deal with those crazy people."

"Angel, those folks who nearly trampled you to death had ...thing to do with this."

Angeline looked up at Gavin, her lavender eyes melting his ...art in a single glance. "What do you mean?"

"I mean, the men who attacked me were paid to do so. They ...re given all the information they needed as to where they ...uld find me and they were well paid to see to it that I couldn't ...erfere with you."

"With me? But who would care whether you talked to me ... not? Who even knew that you were there?" Angeline questioned, her voice raising slightly.

Gavin smiled. "Yes, who knew I was there besides you?

Angeline thought back to that night. "I told Willa. She sa
me after you brought me back to the hotel. She wondere
how I'd managed to escape unharmed and I told her abou
you." Angeline paused and shook her head. "Willa woul
never hire someone to harm you. She'd have no reason."

"Why not, Angel?"

"Like I said, she'd have no reason."

"What did you tell her about me? Think hard," Gavin sai
softly.

Angeline's brows knitted together as she tried to remem
ber. "I told her you were a friend of the family. She asked m
if you were in support of the cause."

"What did you tell her?" Gavin's eyes were intent.

"I told her," Angeline paused, remembering her words wit
some embarrassment.

"Tell me."

"I told her that your cause was getting me to marry you."

"So she'd have no reason to feel threatened. No reason
suspect that I might take you away from her cause?"

Angeline jumped to her feet, mindless of the way she pulle
at Gavin's arm and shoulder as she did. She released his har
indignantly. "I can't believe that Willa would hire hoodlun
to come beat you."

"Calm down, Angel. As far as I could learn, your frie
Douglas Baker is the one who did the hiring." Gavin got
his feet slowly and Angeline took a step back.

"I don't believe you. You're just jealous, that's all."

"Jealous of Baker? Is there something there that merits n
jealousy?" Gavin questioned seriously.

"Douglas is a wonderful man and he isn't at all the ty

at needs to resort to illegal activities. He has powerful friends nd plenty of money. I don't think you would threaten him in he least. As for whether he merits your jealousy, well that imply isn't for me to say." Angeline moved away, unable to ook Gavin in the eye. She knew full well that Douglas was nore than a little interested in her as a woman.

"Angel, I overheard one of the men say that Baker expected o get his money's worth. The others agreed and that's when he man behind me stuck his knife into me."

Angeline turned, a look of shock on her face. Her hand vent to her head. "I can't believe Douglas would be capable f such a thing. It's monstrous."

"If I can give you proof it was Baker, will you realize just ow much danger you're in and come home with me?" Gavin uestioned, moving forward to take hold of her shoulders. he effort caused him to grimace and Angeline stood very ill to keep from further irritating his wounds.

"What kind of proof can you give?" Angeline asked softly.

"What if he admits it himself?" Gavin's fingers played with he wisps of hair at her neck.

"Well of course, that would prove. . . but how in the world re you ever going to get him to just come out and say. . . ." ngeline refused to finish. She shook her head. "He couldn't ave been a part of it."

Gavin's finger traveled up Angeline's neck to her jaw. "Anel, you are such a good-hearted woman. So good-hearted. a fact, that it's difficult for you to believe anyone capable of he kind of evil that lurks in the world."

Angeline relished his warm touch against her skin. She elt her breathing quicken and wondered if Gavin knew how e effected her. How could he? She was only learning about herself.

But Gavin saw the fire in her eyes. He knew she was enjoying being close to him and it gave him hope for their future. "Angel, I'll get the proof, but you didn't answer me. Will you come home with me when I do?"

Angeline was so confident of Douglas' innocence that she saw no reason to withhold her agreement. "If you can show me, beyond any doubt, that Douglas was responsible for your injuries, I'll go home with you." She was lost in his touch and the look in his eyes, but somehow she found the strength to add, "But, if you can't get your proof, will you agree to go home without me?"

Gavin grinned, his eyes twinkling as though he'd already won. "Of course. If I can't prove what I said is true, then I'll leave you to traipse all over the world and I'll even explain to your parents why you didn't return."

"Deal," Angeline said softly.

"Deal."

The clock chimed the hour, breaking the spell. Angeline looked away from Gavin and for the first time realized how very alone they were. "You shouldn't even be here," she said and pulled back. "If anyone finds you here, you'll compromise my reputation."

"That would be a pity," Gavin chuckled. "I might have to marry you then."

Angeline wanted to slug him, but she was too painfully aware of his injuries. "Gavin Lucas, you would try the patience of Job himself."

"So my mother has told me."

"Mine says the same thing about me," Angeline couldn't help but add with a grin. "But even my mother wouldn't approve of you being here with me, like this."

Gavin nodded. "Sorry. I had to see you alone and I didn't

want to risk having Baker see me. Since you two were having such a pleasant dinner, I thought your room would be the safest place to wait."

"But what if he'd accompanied me back here?"

Gavin frown. "Then I would have had to accompany him back downstairs. He'd better never try anything with you, Angel. You belong to me."

Angeline felt both hemmed in and pleased at Gavin's declaration. "I only meant that being a gentleman, he would have seen to my safety and escorted me at least to this floor. Douglas has never tried to impose his will on me. I can't say the same thing for you." Gavin took a step towards her, but Angeline outmanuevered him.

"I make no apologies for my actions, Angel. Your folks like the idea of adding me to the family and my folks adore you. Frankly, I'd appreciate it if you'd give all this up and come home now. I've got a great deal of work waiting for me at the ranch and I've already endured more than I bargained for."

"So go home!" Angeline declared. "You're the only one stopping you. I have no intention of pretending that I want you to stay."

Gavin moved faster than Angeline expected. He swept her into his arms and planted a passionate kiss upon her lips. "Tell me again how you don't want me to stay."

"I don't want you to stay," Angeline said without conviction.

Gavin kissed her again, only longer.

"Tell me."

Angeline's lavender eyes met Gavin's smoky blue ones. "I, uh," she began and saw the amusement on his face at her confusion. "Go home, Gavin."

Gavin lowered his lips to hers once more and this time Angeline kissed him back. "All right!" she declared and forced herself to stepped away from him, breathless and flushed. "I don't want you to go, but I don't want you to cause trouble either."

Gavin laughed, picked up his hat from a nearby chair and cautiously opened the door. "Good seeing you, Angel. Be careful." He started to leave, then pulled back into the room and shut the door. Reaching into his pocket he pulled out a piece of paper. "This is my room number. I'm just one floor down, so if Willa or your precious Douglas try to move you out of town, I'd appreciate it if you'd get word to me."

Angeline took the paper and nodded. "Now, go. Please." She was more disturbed by his kisses than she cared to admit.

"You'll be in my prayers, Angel."

"Thank you," she whispered. "And you'll be in mine."

When Gavin had gone, Angeline sighed and leaned heavily against the door. Her mind raced with thoughts. Could Douglas really have paid to have Gavin beaten? She'd never known Gavin to lie and he'd have no real knowledge of Douglas Baker, otherwise.

"Oh, Lord," she whispered the prayer, "what am I to do? Who can I trust?" Her mind quickly referenced a verse she'd memorized from childhood. Proverbs three, verse five. "Trust in the Lord with all thine heart," she recited, "and lean not unto thine own understanding."

"Everyone is running my life, Father," she said, going to stare out the window. "Gavin comes here with his plans and dreams. He insists I marry him and won't take no for an answer. Willa tells me what to do and say. She makes me read horrible things and tells me what I should feel. She plans my days out in complete detail without ever considering my needs." Angeline smiled to herself when she thought of Gavin's surprise arrival. "Of course, Willa didn't plan on Gavin." Then a thought crossed her mind. She mustn't say anything to give away Gavin's presence. If she told Willa, and Douglas had been responsible for Gavin's attack, she'd end up being the cause of him being hurt further.

With a heavy sigh, she let go of the drapes. "Oh God, please keep him safe. Please don't let them hurt Gavin again."

twelve

The dry, warm days of mountain summer caused Angeline to think of home. She remembered her father and mother with such fondness that she ached at the thought of the distance between them. Despite their differences, they had always shared a closeness that Angeline cherished. It was that obvious void in her life that began to make her rethink her devotion to the cause of suffrage.

Twice she'd made her way to the lobby telephone, but both times she'd stopped herself. If Gavin found the proof he was seeking, then she'd be headed home in a few days anyway. If he didn't find something substantial to prove Douglas' involvement in his attack, then Angeline would give her folks a call and let them know about her trip to Washington D.C.

But Gavin remained mysteriously absent. Angeline had assumed he would spend some time with her now that he was here in Denver. She'd even imagined romantic evenings at the theater or opera with Gavin on her arm. But he never called on her or even so much as sent a message. After nearly a week of this, Angeline began to wonder if he'd admitted defeat and gone home.

"Maybe he couldn't find his proof," she said aloud to herself one day. "At least he could have said good-bye."

The hotel room was more confining as the days passed and Angeline decided an outing was in order. Pulling on her well-worn blue serge skirt, she gave serious thought to her wardrobe. If she stayed on with Willa, she'd have to send for more of her things. Trying to look the part of a smart, young suffragette was most difficult when you had to alternate between three or four changes of clothes.

A knock came at her door and Angeline found her heart skip a beat. Maybe Gavin had come to talk to her again. If so, she'd ask him to accompany her across the street to the lovely park she'd watched for days from her window.

"Who is it?" she called, unlocking the door.

"It's Willa, open up. I have a surprise for you."

Angeline opened the door and greeted her friend. "You certainly seem excited about something. Come on in and tell me all about it."

Willa entered the room with little flair or grace. Instead, she more or less took over a room as a general would claim a piece of ground. "We leave for Washington in two days. The march is already scheduled and the President has agreed to receive us in the White House."

"Two days?" Angeline questioned, uncertain that she could manage on such short notice.

"Yes, is that a problem?"

"Well, I was just considering my clothes," Angeline replied. "You see, I never planned to be away from home more than a week or two. I only have four outfits at best and they are becoming a little worn."

"Ummm," Willa said, surveying Angeline intently. "Yes, it would be appropriate to clothe you better."

"I have a vast wardrobe at home in Bandelero, but I would need to send for my things and there's no real way of knowing whether my folks would send them or not. I have some money, but it certainly isn't enough to refurbish my attire." Angeline's words were straight to the heart of the matter.

"You can't very well show up as one of our best speakers

and look unkept. I'll work on the matter immediately. In the meantime, I've brought you these." Willa pulled out a stack of papers from her valise styled bag.

"What are these and what do you mean 'best speaker'?" Angeline questioned, taking the papers from Willa.

"You have a gift, Angeline. I've already made up your agenda. You will give three speeches while we are in Washington. You will speak first at a small reception where there will be several representatives from each of the forty-eight states. You will speak no longer than ten minutes." Willa motioned Angeline to the table at the far side of the room. "For that occasion, you will give this speech. I just finished writing it for you about an hour ago, so you will need to memorize it and make it characteristically your own."

"I have no intention of speaking, Willa. I'm too new to this," Angeline protested.

"Nonsense. You'll do as you're directed and you will do quite well at it. The next speech will be given at a luncheon for our suffrage association. This again, will last about ten minutes. Here is the speech for that occasion." Willa pointed out the paper and pushed it aside. "Lastly, during our rally at the Capitol, I want you to speak similarly to the way you did in Santa Fe. I tried to recapture the mood and the gist of what you told those people. They were moved to tears there and you will no doubt capture the hearts and minds of many in Washington. You might even catch the national paper's eye and that would truly be a boon to our cause."

Angeline couldn't believe the way Willa had it all planned out. "Do I get any say in this?"

Willa stared at her in mute surprise. "Of course not. I am your mentor, I will teach. You will listen. The time is right for a young, beautiful woman to step forward and help open the eyes of the nation."

"But I'm not even old enough to vote, if we had the vote," Angeline declared.

"It is unimportant. Now you read these over and memorize each and every line. I will get to work on clothing you and will come back this afternoon to see what progress you've made. Don't bother going downstairs for lunch, I'll tell them to send something up." Willa got to her feet and moved to the door. "It is very important to the cause, Angeline, that each of us be prepared."

Angeline remembered Douglas' words about preparation. "I don't mind being prepared," Angeline muttered, "I'd just like a say in what's being prepared for me."

"Pshaw!" Willa denounced her concern. "You're just a child, Angeline. What would you do differently?" Angeline's blank expression gave Willa the fuel she needed to continue. "You know nothing about what is necessary to plan a march or a rally. I have the experience and you don't. It's that simple." With that, Willa was gone before Angeline could even open her mouth to reply.

Angeline did as she was told, although her heart was far from in it. She read the speeches over and over, wondering if she believed any of the words. Women's suffrage had seemed an important cause, but now Angeline just felt used. Used? Wasn't that what Gavin had said they were doing to her?

"Oh, Gavin," she whispered and sighed heavily. "Where are you?" She thought instantly of the hotel room number he'd given her. *Perhaps I should check on him,* Angeline thought to herself. *After all, he was injured. Maybe he's taken a turn for the worse.* She had just gotten to her feet, intent on finding out, when Willa barged in without bothering to knock.

"Well?" she questioned the surprised Angeline. "Have you memorized the speeches?"

"No," Angeline replied in a rather stilted manner.

Willa frowned. "Why not?"

"I haven't had the time for one thing. For another, I'm just not sure I can give these," Angeline said and held up the papers. "They aren't my words. They aren't the way I feel."

"No one needs to know how you feel, except that you demand equal rights for your sisters. Angeline, we've been all through this before."

Angeline plopped down unladylike into the nearest chair. "Willa, I don't even know if I'm going to Washington."

Willa was genuinely taken back by the younger girl's response. "Of course you're going."

Angeline frowned. "Willa, I've tried to be patient about this but I feel like everyone is telling me what to do and no one cares about my feelings. I have parents who are no doubt worried about me and love me. I know they want me to return home and I believe I can remain here and still help suffrage. After all, I have good connections in New Mexico and can write letters. . ."

"Write letters, bah!" Willa interjected. "You need someone like me to teach you. Angeline, you can't keep your head buried in the sand forever. The world is an ugly, cruel place out there and this is war!"

"Yes, exactly," Angeline stated, quieting Willa. "I have two brothers who are in the army. The entire world is waiting to see how the United States will respond to the sinking of the Lusitania and the atrocities in Belgium. It is war and while it very well may be a European war at this point, it could easily become an American interest as well."

"It doesn't matter," Willa protested.

"It does to me! You and Douglas both seem to think you can lead me around on a chain and I will perform like some type of circus animal. Well, I have news for both of you." Even though Angeline spoke Douglas' name, she also thought of Gavin's pushiness. "I have a good mind of my own and I will make my own decisions."

Willa eyed Angeline suspiciously, then gave her a tight-lipped smile. "You're just over tired. Douglas is a good man and he is quite attracted to you. You could do far worse."

"What are you talking about?"

"I think you know very well what I'm talking about," Willa answered. "You are falling in love with Douglas and it frightens you. Douglas would make an excellent husband, so stop fretting."

Angeline's mouth dropped open and for a moment she couldn't say a word. Willa took that as confirmation of her statement. "Douglas Baker is a wealthy, powerful ally and to have you aligned with him in marriage could be quite beneficial to all concerned."

"I have no intention of marrying Douglas Baker!" Angeline exclaimed. "Willa, you must stop this at once. You may look upon me as a child with no will of my own, but my own mother could very well set you straight on that."

Willa held her angry reply and crossed to the door. "Memorize the speeches, Angeline. I'll return in the morning and we will go over the material."

Anger raged up inside of Angeline and as Willa closed the door, she couldn't help but hurl her shoe against it. Unable to think clearly, she took herself to her bedroom and threw herself across the empty bed in order to decide what she should do next.

Angeline never realized how very tired she was. When she awoke the next morning, still fully dressed from the day before, she began to calculate the toll that Willa and the cause were taking on her. She'd barely had time to wash her face and fix her hair when noises sounded from the sitting room, bringing Angeline to investigate.

Willa instructed several bellhops where she wanted them to put the boxes they carried and quietly ushered them from the room with a handful of change to share between them.

"I have your new clothes," she announced unceremoniously. "Try them on and make certain they fit." The order didn't set well with Angeline. Especially in light of the way she'd spent the night.

"Willa, would you please leave. I'm afraid I just woke up and need some time to bathe."

"Nonsense." Willa was already pulling open boxes. "Try this first," she said and tossed a burgundy gown to Angeline.

Angeline caught the heavy satin and held it up to inspect it. "The style is much too old for me," she muttered.

"Your manner of dress is too childish. I want to present a beautiful, sophisticated woman of the world. I want to mold you into an image that women will strive to emulate. Beauty and grace should be synonymous with the suffrage cause and with your help, it will be."

Angeline felt hostile and there was little charity in her words to follow. "You could benefit by your own advice, Willa. You aren't a ugly woman, yet you dress in a mannish style and you wear your hair entirely too severe to look feminine."

Willa was unmoved. "I dress as I do because I have too little time to waste on frills and pampering. You, however, can draw a new generation. These younger women will look to you as a role model. Now go try on the dress."

Angeline did as she was told, quite unhappy that Willa was unwilling to listen to reason.

The gown rustled lightly as Angeline pulled it over her head. The graceful princess lines of the dress were accentuated with painfully narrow stays that would barely allow Angeline room to breath. The cut of the neckline draped alluringly across the bodice and left little question as to the femininity of Angeline's form.

"Come, let me see," Willa called from the sitting room, and obediently, Angeline did as she was told.

Willa nodded in approval. "You look most lovely. There are shoes to match in one of these boxes. You may wear this to the reception."

Angeline could take no more. "Willa, the dress is beautiful, but it isn't me. I would like to have a choice in my clothes and in my itinerary. I want a say in where I go and what I do, not to mention with whom."

"Angeline, we've discussed this before. Now, why don't you try on this white dress?" Willa tried to ignore the fire in Angeline's lavender eyes.

"No!" Angeline stared hard at Willa and put her hands to her hips. "I am not a child to be ordered about. If you want my cooperation in any matter, then you will discuss it with me as an adult. If you do not see fit to treat me in a respectful manner and include me in the planning of situations that involve me, I will return home and forever leave the cause of suffrage behind me."

Willa paled just a bit, but not enough to make Angeline believe she'd taken her seriously. "I mean it, Willa! Stop trying to run my life or I'm going to leave!"

With that Angeline fled from the room and stormed down the hotel hallway, uncertain as to where she would go or what

she should do. Dressed as she was, Angeline drew apprecitive stares from the men on the staircase and it wasn't unt
she'd made it all the way down to the lobby that she knew s
had to return to her room and change.

Grudgingly, she turned and made her way back upstai
What was she going to do and how in the world could s
convince Willa Neal that she was not an ignorant child?

"Lord," she whispered, "I know I've put You alongside
one of my many causes, but I'm starting to see a real need f
a better walk with You. I need a deeper understanding
what You want for my life." Shaking her head and contin
ing the hushed prayer, Angeline wished most adamantly th
she could speak with Gavin.

❧

Gavin had heard the murmurs and hushed comments befo
he'd even glanced up to see what the commotion was all abo
What he saw was rather shocking, but like everyone else
the lobby, he was mesmerized by the vision on the staircas

"Angel!" he whispered and she did seem very much lik
heavenly illusion. Then, much to his amazement, she turne
on the bottom step and rushed back upstairs as though she
forgotten something important.

Gavin got to his feet as if to follow her, but realized
needed to stay put. Douglas Baker was due to join his cr
nies for a drink, at least that's what a well paid bellhop h
passed on to Gavin not fifteen minutes earlier. With the pi
ture of Angeline in the burgundy gown still fresh in his mir
Gavin forced himself to sit back down and wait.

"One of these days, Angel," he breathed almost painful
"One of these days."

thirteen

illa left Angeline's room quickly after the younger girl had
ormed from the premises. She had to find Douglas and talk
him about Angeline. Rather, she had to figure out how
ey could better control Angeline.

Painfully aware of the asset that was about to slip through
r fingers, Willa cautiously made her way to the lobby via
e backstairs. It would do her no good to have another con-
ontation with Angeline just yet. No, it would better to dis-
ss her thoughts with Douglas and see if together they
uldn't get the spirited girl under their control.

The hotel lobby was busy as always. This seemed to be
e of the many gathering places in downtown Denver where
siness deals were made and broke. Willa had chosen the
tel for just such a reason. It never hurt to find oneself rub-
ng elbows with the very powerful and very rich. It cost a
all fortune to maintain the four suites they held here and
illa knew that without Douglas' additional help in the mat-
r she would never have enjoyed the luxury.

Spotting Douglas in his exquisitely tailored suit, Willa ig-
red the men who surrounded him and pleaded with him for
private moment of his time.

"I must say this is a surprise," Douglas said, following Willa
a small sofa in a far corner of the lobby.

There were people everywhere and Willa uncomfortably
anced around her at the nearest occupants to ascertain
hether they could prove harmful. "I'm sorry for the

disruption, Douglas," Willa began, deciding that the peopl
around her were of no consequence. "Angeline is fast be
coming a problem. She had a bit of a fit this morning when
brought her the clothes."

"A beautiful young woman and she got angry at ne
clothes?" Douglas questioned with a chuckle in his voice. "
find that hard to believe."

"Well, believe what you want, but it's true. She's eve
more angry about being told what to do. She wants to ca
her parents, it seems perhaps that friend of hers, you remem
ber the Lucas man? Well, I think perhaps he stirred up fee
ings in her that she can't quite deal with. She hasn't been th
same since he came into the picture."

"I took care of him in New Mexico," Douglas stated flatl
"What more do you want me to do, kill her parents?"

Willa seemed aghast for a moment. It was impossible
tell if Douglas was just saying the words for effect or if h
really meant to offer the solution as a viable possibility.

"Don't give me that shocked expression, Willa. Just cut
the heart of the matter and tell me what you want me to do

"We need better control over Angeline. She's threatene
to walk out. I need her connections and the money behin
them or we'll never get the vote in New Mexico."

"And where do I fit into this?" Douglas questioned, r
membering to keep his voice down.

"Perhaps you would woo the girl and get her to marry yo
As your wife, Angeline would have to respond more respec
fully to instruction." Willa's statement was offered so ma
ter-of-factly that Douglas was now the one silently stunne

Finally, a slow grin spread across his face. "I would ve
much enjoy the pleasure of husbanding Angeline Monro
However, I doubt very seriously that you could convince h

agree."

"I'm not suggesting you ask her, but rather you tell her. Force her if necessary. Use the threat of her parents. It doesn't matter. If you have her under control, then we can get at her connections."

"Angeline doesn't strike me as the kind of girl who will be easily swayed by idle threats," Douglas replied.

"Then don't make idle threats!"

Willa's voice rose enough to cause Douglas to glance around at the nearby hotel guests. No one seemed interested in their other lively conversation, however. In fact, the man directly across from them was thoroughly engrossed in a copy of the *Denver Post* and seemed not to even notice that other people occupied the same room.

"Look," Douglas whispered. "I'll do what I can. I also could use Angeline's connections as you well know. But I'm going to have to persuade her to marry me and perhaps that will result in her spending less time involved in the suffrage cause and more time on my arm."

"I can't give her up to you," Willa declared firmly.

"What do you think you would be doing if she married me?" Douglas questioned. "Did you think I'd invite you on the honeymoon?" His face was twisted in a leering expression.

"Don't be vulgar with me!"

"Then don't be foolish in your dealing with me. I will get Angeline to marry me, but there is price to pay, my dear, dear Willa. You may control the child to a degree, but after we are married she's mine and everything she does must come through me first. That includes the suffrage cause and any political contacts you make through her."

Willa considered the words for a moment and nodded. "Very

well. If we are to be adversaries for her attentions, at least l[
us be cooperative ones."

"Rather like the United States and Germany and this i[
sane agreed upon neutrality?"

"Neutrality serves my purpose very well," Willa stated a[
got up to leave. "I'd rather we never enter war and take t[
focus away from the rights of women in this nation."

Douglas got to his feet. "You seem rather unconcerned wi[
the rights of one particular woman," he said with a smirk. [
doubt you'd ever tolerate such a heavy hand upon your will[

"Just bring her under control, Douglas."

"So that she responds more respectfully to instruction[
Douglas used Willa's words against her.

Willa's eyes narrowed and Douglas realized quickly that [
wasn't best to have this powerful suffragette against him. [
least not in this manner. "Just see to it, Douglas."

"Certainly, madam," he said with a slight bow. "May I e[
cort you somewhere?"

"No, I have a meeting nearby." With that Willa went o[
direction and Douglas the other and neither saw Gavin low[
his newspaper with an intent look of concern edging his fe[
tures.

"If this weren't becoming just a little too dangerous for m[
taste," Gavin muttered, folding the newspaper under h[
arm,"I'd like to see Baker try to tame Angel. What a laugh[

"Did you say something, sir?" A hotel attendant was quick[
at his side.

"Yes," Gavin replied and thrust the newspaper at the ma[
"Dispose of this for me, please." The man quickly took t[
paper, while Gavin made his way to the main staircase.

I'd better warn Angel, he thought. Taking the steps two [
time, he glanced quickly over his shoulder to assure hims[

at Douglas Baker was still moving towards the men's club
atryway. Noting that he was, Gavin slowed his step a bit
ad tried to figure out a plan.

*Angel will be suspicious no matter what I say, so I'd best
ust come clean with the truth.* Gavin reasoned that he'd
ave certain information to give Angeline that would prove
e'd overheard Douglas and Willa in conversation. Perhaps
at would be enough, he tried to convince himself.

Making his way to Angeline's room, Gavin began to pray
earnest. "Father, she's so innocent and she doesn't begin
understand what these people are trying to do to her," he
hispered the words under his breath. "Please help me to
onvince her. Please show me a way to reveal the true nature
f these people, so that she won't be hurt by their scheming,
men."

He finished the prayer just as he reached Angeline's door.
nocking for several minutes, with worried glances down
e hall toward the stairs, Gavin finally gave up and tried to
ink where Angeline might have gone.

Heading down the backstairs, Gavin immediately thought
f the park across the street. Angel would love it there! He
ced down the remaining steps and made his way to the park.
he just had to be there, he thought. "Please God, let me find
er first."

&

ngeline had found the confines of her room unsettling and
ore than once had hoped for a stroll in the city park across
om the hotel. Willa's absence from her room had allowed
er to change out of the very grown-up burgundy satin and
to her serviceable blue serge skirt and shirtwaist. Before
e realized what she was doing, Angeline found herself stroll-
g among the park's aspens and pines as though she'd been

there a hundred times before.

It was summertime, soon to be heading into fall an
Angeline marveled at the colorful flower beds. Carefully cul
tivated rosebushes were in full bloom and the scent tha
lingered on the warm air was heavenly. Taking a seat on
nearby park bench, Angeline wondered what she was to do
On one hand, she wanted to be helpful to the cause of secur
ing women the right to vote. But, on the other hand, she knev
that Willa's ideals and forceful ways were not her style. Fur
thermore, Angeline knew they were not God's ways either.

"I hoped I'd find you here," the familiar voice called ou
and Angeline didn't know whether to be relieved or concerned

"Hello, Gavin," she replied and looked up to find his gaz
fixed on her. My, but he was a welcome sight!

"You look a little upset. Want to talk about it?"

"No," Angeline stated emphatically.

"Well, I do." Gavin took a seat beside her and put his arı
around her.

Angeline stared at him hard for a moment, but when Gavin'
grin only broadened, she stiffened her shoulders and sat o
the edge of the bench.

"You can't get comfortable that way," Gavin teased.

"It wouldn't be appropriate for me to sit beside you lik
that." Angeline nodded backwards toward his arm.

"But we're engaged," he argued.

"It doesn't matter. It still isn't appropriate," Angeline a
swered and only after it was too late, realized that she'd a
firmed Gavin's possession of her.

Gavin wasn't shy about grasping onto the words for sec
rity. "So maybe we should set the date."

Angeline glared at him and scooted away from him. "Hav
you found the proof you need?"

"Yes, as a matter of fact," Gavin said, causing Angeline to drop her stuffy look. "I see that surprises you."

"Well, I suppose it does. Well, maybe not surprise, oh, I don't know." Her hands went to her head as if she could sort everything into prospective with wave of her hand.

Gavin pulled her back against him and forced her to remain. "Don't go, Angel. We need to talk. You're in danger and I have to warn you in order to keep you from making a very grave mistake."

"What do you mean, I'm in danger?" she questioned and stopped her struggles.

"Willa wasn't very happy that you didn't like the new clothes," Gavin stated and Angeline gasped at the words. "I see that verifies for you that I have a reliable source. Matter of fact, this time it came straight from the horse's mouth." He grinned hard. "So to speak. Of course, I thought you looked real nice in that little red number."

"Burgundy," Angeline muttered without realizing until too late the compliment he was paying her.

"It was a little out of your routine style of dress, but I thought it looked great." His warm breath was against her ear and his words were so soft and alluring that Angeline found herself nearly hypnotized. Nearly, but not quite.

"When did you see me in that dress?" she asked quietly, trying to steady the racing of her heart.

"When you came storming downstairs. My, oh my, but you did look fit to be tied." Gavin was laughing softly and Angeline jabbed him quickly in the ribs.

"Why am I supposed to be in danger and why should I believe anything you say?"

"I've been trying to get the proof you asked me for, remember? Well I was sitting in the lobby when Douglas Baker and your friend, Willa Neal, came sauntering over to where I was and began talking about the need to control you."

Startled at his words, Angeline jerked away and stared at Gavin. "You were sitting right there and they didn't see you?"

"Nope, I had the paper in front of my face the whole time. Anyway," Gavin began again and paused. "Are you listening to this, Angel? I don't want to have to repeat myself."

"I'm listening. Just get on with it."

"Well, it seems Miss Neal is quite worried about you and your political associates slipping away. Seems you threatened the old woman that if she didn't stop interfering and planning your life you were going home."

Angeline nodded. "I did say that, so I guess I should believe that what you say is true."

Gavin looked hurt. "I've never lied to you, Angel."

"No, I suppose you wouldn't, even to get me back home," she responded, sorry that she'd hurt his feelings.

The seriousness of Gavin's expression only deepened. "Angel, Willa Neal wants you to marry Douglas Baker. He's going to try to court you and get you to marry him right away. Miss Neal even suggested force." He wasn't about to tell her that this included the death of her parents in that threat.

"Oh really, Gavin!" she exclaimed and got to her feet. "You must be over-exaggerating. Douglas has no interest in me outside of the political arena." She faced him with her hands on her hips and eyes fairly blazing. "I know you mean well, but this is too much."

One minute Gavin was seated on the bench with that all-knowing look that Angeline had come to know better than to argue with and the next minute he'd pulled her into his arms.

"Angel, you have to listen to reason." His voice was nearly hoarse with pent emotion. "I love you and I know you love me, too. You're just too pig-headed to admit to your feelings and leave this nonsense behind. They're using you and I can't stand by and let that American kaiser dictate to you how you'll spend the rest of your life. Marry me, Angel. Come away with me and marry me now." Before she could speak, Gavin lowered his lips to hers and tenderly kissed her. It was a kiss like no other Angeline had ever known. And though her experience was quite limited, she found the urgency in his manner most confusing.

Slumping against his chest and letting him support her full weight, Angeline nearly broke into tears. What was she to do? Had Gavin spoken the truth? Of course he had, she chided herself. She'd never known him to lie, but if he hadn't lied then that meant Willa and Douglas cared nothing about her as a person. Feeling Gavin's arms tighten around her, Angeline knew the blunt, harsh reality of what he'd shared. Gavin's truth was no different than the conclusions she'd already come to.

"Let me take you away from here, Angel. You belong with me."

❧

From the seclusion of his hiding place, Douglas Baker snapped a twig in half. The scowl on his face was enough to distinguish his mood had his actions not already made that clear. He found it hard to believe he was witnessing Angeline in the arms of that Lucas man. Hadn't he paid well enough to have Lucas out of the picture, permanently?

"I won't be so gracious next time, Lucas," Douglas muttered and watched as Gavin kissed Angeline. Dropping his hand from where it divided the brush, Douglas turned back toward the pathway and made his plans. "I'll put an end to this entire charade, once and for all." His words were low enough to offer comfort to their speaker, but not loud enough to give away his plans.

"I'll teach Willa Neal the meaning of respectful response to instructions," Douglas announced, emerging from the park with a plan already formulating in his mind. "I'll teach them all."

fourteen

Angeline was nearly back to her room when she spotted a red-clad bellhop knocking on her door.

"May I help you?" she asked.

"Are you Miss Angeline Monroe?"

"Yes, I am."

"Then this is for you." He handed her a folded piece of paper.

The note read: *Please meet me in the hotel restaurant in fifteen minutes.* It was signed, *Elaine Cody.*

"Who is Elaine Cody?" Angeline wondered and folded the note and handed the bellhop a nickel from her skirt pocket.

"Not sure, ma'am," the young man replied, "but she said it was urgent."

"I see," Angeline said thoughtfully. "Please tell her I'll be there." The boy nodded and took off down the hall.

Angeline pulled her key out and entered her room. A quick glance revealed no sign of an intruding Willa or anyone else, and for that Angeline breathed a sigh of relief. It seemed of late that nearly everyone had a way in and out of her room.

Deciding to quickly freshen up, Angeline went to the wardrobe. A survey of the clothes hanging there revealed that Willa had once again mettled in Angeline's affairs. None of Angeline's original clothes remained, forcing her to either continue wearing the serge skirt and shirtwaist or give in and utilize the new attire.

Stomping her foot in a private protest, Angeline muttered

117

to herself and fingered through the dresses. Willa had thoughtfully provided for her daytime needs as well as evening wear. Choosing a sedate forest green suit, Angeline didn't stop grumbling about the interference until she reached the bottom step of the grand staircase.

Angeline was led to the table where Elaine Cody waited. "Miss Monroe," the woman said motioning her to take a seat.

Elaine Cody was a simple woman in her thirties. She wore her brown hair short and curled and a simple gown of lavender and cream. "Are you hungry?"

Angeline smiled. "I've had such a busy day that I hadn't even thought to eat." She took the chair across from Elaine. "I hope I don't sound rude, but I don't know why you've called me here, Miss Cody."

"Mrs. Cody," the woman said sweetly. "I know this is a surprise, but we've been trying for several weeks to talk to you, but Willa Neal always managed to put a stop to it."

"Why would Willa keep us from talking?"

"I represent a less radical approach to the suffrage movement," Elaine said softly. She paused long enough to allow Angeline to order something to eat when the waiter approached their table. When the man had graciously left the table, Elaine continued.

"Willa Neal and her comrades believe that change can only come through militant action. They've caused civil upheaval all across the nation, even the world. On the other hand, our organization believes that a direct, but less radical approach is the best."

"I must say I do agree, Mrs. Cody."

"Please call me Elaine."

"And you must call me Angeline."

"Angeline, Willa Neal does more to harm the cause of

suffrage than to aid it. She gives people the impression that all suffrage supporters are violent in nature and care nothing for legal processes. Suffrage is an important, no, a vital issue, but we can win this cause through rational, straightforward behavior and by educating people to the importance of women voting."

Elaine's words mirrored Angeline's thoughts exactly. "I have long felt," Angeline began, pausing only to accept the lobster salad that the waiter placed in front of her, "that Willa's approach often worries me. I was with her in New Mexico when the crowd stormed the stage. It was terrifying. Willa seems to enjoy stirring people up, however, and she won't hear reason from me."

"Perhaps you would consider attending one of our functions," Elaine said with a smile. She was glad to hear that Angeline appreciated a less militant approach to suffrage.

Angeline shared her smile. "I think it would a welcome change, but I'm leaving soon for Washington. Willa has a march on the Capitol planned and a meeting with the President."

"Yes, I know," Elaine replied. "Maybe you should reconsider your plans, however." Elaine grew thoughtful for a moment. "I don't know how to say this without sounding rather trite, but do you realize that Willa preys on people like you?"

Angeline put down her fork. "What do you mean?"

Elaine shifted uncomfortably. "You have friends or at least your family has friends who can offer Willa and her cause a great deal of support and money."

"And you believe that Willa's sole interest in my participation is that I join her with these friends?"

"I'm sorry, but I've seen her at work before. You have to remember Colorado has had suffrage for many years. Willa

Neal actively pursued the vote for women and even then she wasn't opposed to breaking the law. She uses whoever she can and always she weighs the benefit of each participant before she pulls them into her circle."

Angeline's frown and sudden lack of appetite caused Elaine to reach her hand out to Angeline's arm. "I am sorry, but it is important that you know what you're up against. Willa is looking for power. Unfortunately, she doesn't care who she uses, nor what happens to them when she's accomplished what she's set out to do."

Just then the waiter came with a silver tray holding a piece of paper. "Excuse me, but I have a message for Miss Monroe."

"I'm Miss Monroe," Angeline said, reaching for the note.

Angeline scanned the note quickly. It was from Gavin and he requested that she join him immediately in the lobby. How was it that he always seemed to know where she was?

"I'm afraid something has come up, Elaine. A friend of mine has asked me to join him and says that it can't wait. I hope you will excuse me."

"Of course," Elaine replied. "I hope we have a chance to speak again."

Angeline nodded. "I hope so too." She turned to the waiter. "Please put this luncheon on Miss Willa Neal's account." She winked at Elaine with a knowing smile.

Making her way through the dining hall, Angeline searched the lobby for Gavin. People seemed to occupy every corner of the busy lobby, but Gavin was nowhere in sight.

"Looking for me, Angel?" Gavin whispered from behind her.

"What's wrong?" she asked in a worried tone. She looked Gavin over in case he'd once again come into harm. Seeing he was unhurt, Angeline relaxed a bit.

Nice to know you can come quickly when you're called."
grinned mischievously at her and took her arm in his hand.
u look real nice, Angel. More new clothes?"

Yes." She sounded irritated and Gavin raised a brow in
stion. "Willa took all of my clothes and left me with these."
You still have that red one?"

Burgundy," Angeline corrected again, but this time she
ldn't help but smile. "You kind of liked that one, eh?"

avin's grin broadened. "Kind of." He pulled her along
him to a closed, ornate wood door. "Do you know what's
ere?"

I have no idea," she replied dryly and added, "but I'm
you're going to tell me."

This is the men's private smoking lounge. Women are
ctly forbidden entry."

How nice," Angeline said, trying to sound offended.

avin pulled her closer. "Baker and his men are seques-
d in there. I believe, if I may offer a guess, that they are
ining how to force you into marriage. I think perhaps, if I
get you close enough, you will overhear the proof you
t of Baker's guilt."

ngeline paled only a bit, but it was enough to make Gavin
concern for the younger woman. "I promise I won't let
hurt you, Angel."

How are you going to get me in there?" she asked softly,
dying herself on Gavin's arm. "I thought women weren't
wed."

I have a plan," he said with uncustomary seriousness.
me on."

ngeline let Gavin take her along a servant's corridor. A
se of anticipation and dread seemed to hang over her.

Wasn't this her moment of truth? No, she thought, she'd ready come to believe what Gavin had told her as true. ? put her hand out to stop Gavin from opening the door.

"You don't have to do this," she whispered, her laven eyes seeking his.

Gavin understood at once what she was saying. "Just once," he said softly and touched his finger to her che "Just this once I will give you absolute proof of what I you to be true. Then, in the future, when I give you my w on a matter, you will remember this and not doubt me."

Angeline suddenly felt a cold chill. "No," she said ag as Gavin slowly turned the doorknob.

"Where's your spunk, Angel?"

The room was dimly lit and the low rumbling of male vo rose up with the assaulting cigar smoke. Gavin held Ange tightly to his side and moved slowly through the storage ro where crates of whiskey were carefully concealed in woo boxes marked "Medical Supplies."

Angeline's eyes gradually adjusted to the light and she in her surroundings with a great deal of interest. The ro was paneled in a dark walnut with brass fixtures and eme green draperies. "So this is where men come to get av from women," she mused. "What do they talk about w they get here?"

Gavin chuckled low. "Women, of course." Angeline sta to giggle, but Gavin quickly clamped his hand over her mo "Shhh." He lowered his hand and pointed to where a n sive plant blocked a clear view of the occupants behin "Baker." Angeline's eyes widened as Gavin pulled her ther behind the plant and held her close.

"You took your time getting here," Douglas was say Angeline couldn't see who he was talking to, but she y much aware of Gavin's arm around her waist.

We're here, ain't we? What'da you want?"

Yeah," a second voice chimed in. "What'da ya want?"

We have a particular matter that I want taken care of,"
uglas began. "It's a problem I thought I'd rid myself of in
w Mexico."

One of those pain-in-neck women?"

No," Douglas replied. "A man. His name is Lucas. Gavin
:as. I hired some local thugs to put him out of my misery
they failed to do the job right."

ngeline nearly gasped at the casual way Douglas spoke
rying to have Gavin incapacitated, but she caught herself
ime and put her hand over her mouth.

So you want us to finish the job?"

That's right. I thought it could be dealt with, without hav-
to be permanent, but I was wrong. He's staying here in
hotel. I have his room number and a pass key. Take care
t tonight."

Sure Baker, but it'll cost you extra."

You'll have your money when the job's done," Douglas
lied. "After Lucas is out of the way, we're going to put an
l to Miss Neal's planned Washington trip. The last thing
need is a bunch of addle-brained women marching on the
pitol."

Thought you supported their votin' cause." one of the men
l with a laugh.

I'm the only cause I support. Giving women the right to
e is like giving them a purse full of money. They won't
w how to handle it properly and they'll only ask for more
:e that's gone."

ngeline forgot herself and pushed away from Gavin to
front Douglas. "How dare you! How dare you sit here

plotting to end a man's life and ruin the efforts of an enti
movement!"

Douglas' eyes registered his surprise, but his tone indicat
nothing out of the ordinary had happened. "Angeline, y
would have been wise to stay out of this." He sounded like
parent scolding a child. "And you, Mr. Lucas, you shou
have learned your lesson in New Mexico."

Angeline hadn't even realized that Gavin had joined h
"You leave Gavin out of this. He was only doing what n
parents asked him to do. You had no right to interfere in n
life that way, Douglas."

"I had every right. Now if you'll calm down, perhaps v
could discuss this more privately. Say upstairs."

"I don't want to discuss this with anyone but the approp
ate authorities," Angeline stated angrily. She felt streng
ened by Gavin's presence, certain that no harm could pos
bly come to them here.

The seclusion of Douglas' table worked to his advanta
No one seemed close enough to be able to overhear the co
motion and even if they could, people here weren't given
interfering in one another's business. With a nod at his co
panions, rough looking characters who made Angeline tak
step back, Douglas got to his feet.

"And what proof will you offer?" Douglas questioned, st
ing intently into Angeline's eyes.

"My word will be good enough for starts. I'll call
Jefferson Ashton and he'll help me in whatever I need." S
turned to ask Gavin to take her to her room, but Doug
stopped her with an iron-like grasp on her arm. Gavin reach
out to free Angeline, but Douglas pushed something cold a
hard into his ribs. "I have a gun trained on your you
man, Angeline. Please tell him it would be wise to do thin

y way."

The two men with Douglas stood up and produced their wn weapons. Angeline turned ashen and nodded her coop-ation, while Gavin grit his teeth and stared daggers into aker.

"Good," Douglas said when he saw they were going to operate. "Now let's go upstairs and talk about this like tional adults."

fifteen

"Where should we take them?" Douglas asked one of th[e] ruffians.

"We still got that room up on three," the man replied.

"Good," Douglas said with a satisfied smile. "Let's g[o] there." He pushed Angeline in front of him, then took hold [of] her with one hand and steadied the gun between them. "No[w] Mr. Lucas, I won't have any problem from you, will I?"

Douglas made certain Gavin could see the gun. "You wo[n't] have any trouble with me." Gavin's voice was deadly in i[ts] tone.

"Douglas, this is ridiculous," Angeline protested. "This is[n't] the old West. You can't simply walk up to people and p[ut] guns on them. Why even back in Bandelero, as primitive as [it] can be, people don't walk around doing this."

"Dear, sweet child," Douglas said, tightening his grip [on] her arm, "keep your voice down, or my good friends are g[o]ing to put an end to your good friend."

Angeline paled and felt her heart pound harder. She could[n't] let Douglas hurt Gavin, no matter the cost. She steadied h[er] nerves and lowered her voice to a whisper. "He's got nothi[ng] to do with this. If you don't like the suffrage movement, de[al] with Willa or even me, but leave Gavin out of it."

"Mr. Lucas has become, shall we say, a personal challeng[e]," Douglas replied and turned a leering smile on Angeline. "B[ut] never fear, I do intend to deal with Willa and my plans f[or] you are more promising with every passing moment."

126

Gavin growled from behind them and moved at Douglas as f to separate him from Angeline. "I wouldn't do that, Mr. ,ucas," Douglas said quite seriously. "If this gun accidently ,oes off, guess who's hands the police will find it in?"

"Don't push him, Gavin," Angeline said in a pleading voice. Please don't risk it."

Gavin backed off, feeling the presence of the other two men t his side. Douglas led the way, pulling Angeline along as ough they were sweethearts. Together, the strange looking roup made their way through the smoking room and into the bby. Crossing the room cautiously, Douglas motioned in e direction of one of the back staircases and the men nod-ed and prodded Gavin to follow.

Angeline tried to think of something to do or say, but Dou-las seemed comfortable and far too familiar with the gun at he occasionally nudged into her side.

Lord, she prayed, *there's no one but You to help us. Please ather, Gavin and I need your mercy.* Angeline climbed the st set of stairs, feeling a bit light-headed. The altitude had ttle to do with it. This dizzy feeling came from fear. Fear at if something in Angeline and Gavin's favor didn't hap-en soon, someone was going to get hurt. If not killed.

I should have gone home with Gavin when he first found e, Angeline thought to herself. She glanced over her shoul-er to catch Gavin's eyes. It rallied her heart a bit, just to see at he was so near and very much alive.

One of Douglas' men unlocked the door and shoved Gavin , while Douglas walked through casually. With Angeline ill on his arm, Douglas pointed to a nearby chair. "Sit there, ucas. Joe, tie him up."

Gavin stared at Baker for a moment. His steely blue eyes emed to darken to black and Angeline saw an anger in him that she'd never known him capable of. "You'd better not hurt her," Gavin growled.

"That, my dear Mr. Lucas, is entirely up to you. If you behave yourself and do as you're told, then Angeline will remain perfectly well." Douglas paused and ran his finger along Angeline's jaw, further tormenting Gavin.

Clenching his fists at his side, Gavin took a seat and allowed the men to tie him to the chair. His eyes never left Douglas Baker, however.

"Now, gag him," Baker said and pointed Angeline to an empty chair. "Sit there, my dear. We're going to discuss our wedding."

"Our what!?"

"You heard me. Sit."

Angeline stared in disbelief at Douglas, but it was Gavin's words that calmed her. "Easy, Angeline. Just remember God's the One Who's in control—not Baker and not Willa."

Angeline's head quickly went to the source and met Gavin's eyes for reassurance. The hope went out of her at the sight of Gavin's captivity. *Oh, this is all my fault!* She wanted to say the words, but wouldn't give Douglas the satisfaction.

"I thought I told you to gag him," Douglas said and pushed Angeline to the chair. The men produced a strip of material and gagged Gavin's mouth, while Douglas addressed Angeline.

"Now, let's get to the heart of the matter. It seems you've placed me in an awkward position, but it isn't without its remedies."

"I'm going to see that you get what's coming to you!" Angeline said, angrily twisting away from Douglas.

"That's my plan," Douglas grinned and pulled a chair beside her. "You and I are going to get married, Angeline."

"Never! I'll never marry you!"

"Never is a frightfully long time, my dear. Now, the way I see it," he paused and motioned her to look at Gavin, "our friend over there is in need of your utmost cooperation. If you don't marry me and keep what you know to yourself, I will see to it that he dies."

The words left Angeline cold. She couldn't take her eyes from Gavin and even though he shook his head at her, she knew there was no other choice.

"And if I marry you, what proof do I have that you won't kill him anyway?"

Douglas smiled. "We need each other, Angeline. You need me to keep my word and allow your Mr. Lucas to live. I need you to keep your mouth shut and to get me the support of your New Mexican politician friends. Now, once we're married, I will release Mr. Lucas. I will, of course, keep track of his whereabouts, just in case you decide to share any secrets with Willa. Should that unfortunate thing happen, I will send one of these gentlemen to even the score. You might try to ruin me, Angeline, but just remember," Douglas voice lowered to barely a whisper, "you'll already be my wife. There won't be any way you can escape."

Gavin made noises from behind his gag, but Douglas only seemed to enjoy his agony. "That's right, Mr. Lucas, she will be my wife. That is, if your life means anything at all to her and I can clearly see that it does."

Gavin grew quiet, his eyes narrowing in on Baker. It wasn't the first time Douglas had seen death in the eyes of a man. A man who very much wanted that death to be his own. It unsettled Baker for only a moment.

"Do you plan to kill Willa, as well?"

Angeline's words brought Douglas' attention back to her.

"Kill her? No. That would be a waste of time. The woman is only one step away from an asylum. I'll see her put away where she belongs. I'll also see an end to this infernal suffrage movement."

"I thought you supported the cause," Angeline said, hoping he'd forget about the marriage idea. "What changed your mind?"

"I've never supported women having the vote," Douglas said simply. "I saw a group of people I could benefit from and I ran the risk of associating myself with their cause. Causes are stepping stones for me, Angeline. They mean very little," he paused, "except in relationship to how they can benefit me."

Angeline felt as though she'd been slapped. It was exactly the same way she'd perceived causes. Was it possible that others saw her as distasteful and dishonest as she now saw Douglas? With her brows knitted together thoughtfully, she looked at Gavin who seemed to understand her sudden revelation. It was like growing up ten years in one single moment.

Angeline looked away, unable to meet Gavin's eyes. *I've only sought to benefit myself,* she thought. *I've run from one cause to another, including Christianity, and now I've nothing.* Angeline was miserable. Then a still, small voice stirred inside her.

It isn't true. You have God. You have the foundations of the faith you were born to. Reach out to Him. Trust His guidance.

Angeline squared her shoulders. "I have a headache, Douglas. Would you please get on with this. What is it that you expect me to do now?"

Douglas seemed quite pleased with her seeming acquiescence. "We will announce it to Willa, of course. She'll be quite pleased, you know. She's the one who originally put me onto the idea of marrying you. I saw the potential and decided it was a wise suggestion."

"So we just go to her now and announce it?" Angeline was trying not to let anything Douglas said effect her one way or the other. *I have to keep my head,* she thought. *I have to remain calm or they will kill Gavin.*

"I don't see why not. I know she'll want to be a part of it."

"Very well, Douglas," Angeline said and got to her feet. She refused to look at Gavin for fear she'd break down. "Let's find her."

Douglas was surprised, but pleasantly so, at Angeline's sudden cooperation. After weeks of seeing her as a naive child, however, he was very much mistaken in his assessment of her attitude. What Douglas believed was her childish nature accepting the inevitable was what Gavin recognized to be Angeline's way of preparing for war.

"My, but this is exciting," Willa said with a broad smile and a knowing glance at Douglas. Angeline saw the exchange, but chose to ignore it and play dumb. *If they think I'm a simpleton,* Angeline thought to herself, *so much the better.*

Angeline tried to smile and appear excited. "Douglas is so spontaneous," she said as eagerly as she could. "He wants us to marry right away."

"But of course!" Willa declared and embraced Angeline, who stared menacingly at Douglas over the older woman's back. "This is big," Willa announced. "Really big. We must make it public."

"I don't understand," Angeline replied. "What is it that you have in mind?"

"A public wedding!" Willa's mind was already making

preparations. "We'll put off the Washington trip. I received word today that President Wilson couldn't meet with us anyway."

This was the very thing Douglas wanted and Angeline noted the pleasure in his eyes as he came to stand beside her. "Of course, money is no object," he said smugly. "My family will be happy to. . ."

"No, no, no," Willa interrupted him. "This is much bigger than that. I'll speak with Jefferson Ashton. He's a good friend of Angeline's family and can probably arrange something with the Governor."

Douglas nodded, yielding to the older woman's wisdom, while Angeline remained silent. She was plotting in her mind how she could rescue Gavin and escape Douglas' plans.

"Are you all right, my dear?" Douglas' charming concern was almost too much for Angeline to stomach.

"It's my headache. I can't seem to be rid of it."

"Douglas, take this poor child to her room. You and I can plan the details of this event."

"Certainly, Willa," he said with a smile that revealed his perfect teeth. "I wouldn't want my bride-to-be to come down with something serious."

Angeline batted her eyes at Douglas as though he could hang the moon and the stars in the sky, making Willa laugh.

"I knew you two were made for each other," she said with an undercurrent of mastery in her voice.

"That you did, Willa," Douglas said knowingly. He took hold of Angeline's arm and led her to the door. "I'll be free in a few minutes. Perhaps you would take dinner with me downstairs?"

"That would be fine, Douglas. I'll meet you there," Willa replied.

Angeline remained silent until Douglas had walked her down the hall to her suite. "Why do you hate suffrage so? Willa has worked very hard for the cause and whether she believes in it for all the right reasons or not, it is worthy of passage."

"You are dangerously naive, Angeline," Douglas answered, taking her key and unlocking the door. Handing it back to her, he closed his hand over hers. "Soon, we'll share a room."

Angeline wanted to smash her foot down on his, but instead she lowered her eyes as though embarrassed. In truth, she was, but it wasn't something she'd ordinarily have allowed Douglas to see.

"Why is it not worthy of passage?" she asked again.

Douglas was unconcerned with the way she ignored his suggestive words. "Suffrage is only the start, Angeline. I am a futurist. I see down the road and know the turn of events that will come to pass, by those that have already happened."

"No one can see the future. Only God has that power."

"God may well have made the future, but He isn't the only one who can see it coming."

"For example?" Angeline questioned.

"War," Douglas replied and Angeline's spine tingled.

"War?" Her voice was shaky, her face clearly pale.

"Yes. We'll be involved in the European war soon. Probably before next year is out, although since it is an election year for Wilson and overall the people love the fact that he's kept us neutral, it might be 1917 before we actually get around to it."

"What else?" Angeline felt that she needed to know what Douglas could see. After all, maybe he was right.

"We'll win it, of course. But it will be bloody and senseless. Some will make a great deal of money on it and others will suffer for it. When it's all said and done, I predict a great deal of prosperity for this country and I intend to be in on it from the start."

"What about suffrage?"

"Unfortunately," Douglas said with a faraway look in his eyes, "I believe that unless I can stop this thing now, it will get out of hand and passage will be accomplished."

"And would that be so bad?"

"It would be a nightmare. It's bad enough they gave slaves and Indians the right to voting. Look what that's brought us to."

"And what is that?"

"They want more rights of course. The Indians whine to the President that they deserve, as voting Americans, to have back more land. They argue about land that their ancestors held and the way the white man has taken it from them. If women were given the right to vote, what would they want next?"

"I'm sure I don't know," Angeline replied evenly. "Perhaps they would strive to marry for love and not because someone, some man, arranged to force it upon them.

"Perhaps," Douglas smiled. "But then again, woman are like children. You need a good pat on the head when you behave properly," he said and did just that to Angeline. "And a firm hand otherwise when they step out of line."

"I see," Angeline said in a stilted voice.

"I'm glad you do," Douglas said and dropped his hand from where he'd rested it casually on her shoulder, "because Gavin Lucas' life depends on you."

Angeline entered her room and closed the door gently. Leaning hard against it, she began to cry. At first the tears just welled up in her eyes, but soon she was sobbing and there was no turning off the water.

"What do I do?" she cried and threw herself down into a chair. Her hand fell across the table and beneath it she felt the Bible and suddenly knew what she had to do.

sixteen

The Bible fell open to the fifteenth chapter of Luke and
Angeline immediately read the story of the Prodigal Son. She
saw herself in the selfishness of the prodigal. She felt the
heaviness of guilt weigh her down as she read of the childish
demands the boy had placed on his father.

"I placed so many demands on my parents," she whispered
and wiped at her tears with the back of her sleeve.

Continuing to read, Angeline watched the tale unfold much
like her own. The boy had gone away to a far off land, in
order to live as he wanted. Then one day the joy of it was
gone and there was nothing left and that was exactly how
Angeline felt.

She thought for a moment of Gavin facing death, knowing
that he couldn't help himself, and she shivered. "I have to
help him, Lord." She looked up at the ceiling and wondered
if God even bothered to listen to her anymore.

"The prodigal repented," Angeline whispered and moved
her gaze back to the Bible. "I will arise and go to my father,
and will say unto him, Father, I have sinned against heaven,
and before thee," the eighteenth verse said. Nineteen continued, "I am no more worthy to be called thy son: make me as
one of thy hired servants."

Angeline paused and tears anew streamed from her eyes.
"I'm not worthy," she said with a moan. "I've followed God
only because it suited my purpose to do so. It was my cause
and I wore it proud, but it means nothing. Oh God," she whis-

ed and threw herself to her knees. With hand clasped to-
her she raised them heavenward. "Please forgive me! I
ow how wrong I've been. I see it all now. When I was
ung it was a game to play. I went to church because that
s the place to be seen. I played at being good, because
t's what people expected. I mocked You and Your service,
wever, and I don't deserve forgiveness, but I plead for it."
She sobbed into her hands, her heart nearly tearing in two
m the admission of all that had gone along in the past. "I
a vain and prideful woman, Father. I also sought my will
t and never considered what other people wanted. I cer-
ly never considered what You might want. And now. . . ."

couldn't say it. She couldn't bring herself to imagine that
·n now Gavin might already lie dead in some dark alley-
y.

I love him, Father. Oh, I really, really do. I couldn't see
w much, until. . .until. . . ." She looked at her hands and felt
helplessness and hopelessness threaten to swallow her.
h, God, help him. Take me, but don't let them kill Gavin."
·e thought of her words for a moment, then knew without a
ibt that she meant them with all of her heart.

Yes, Lord," she nodded, suddenly more sedate, "take my
, if a life must be given, but please spare Gavin. I can't
ir it that I've put him in this position. He wouldn't be here
t weren't for his love for me. Now, Father, I realize my
·e for him and I want to exchange places with him. You
t Your Son Jesus, to take my place on the cross, so I know
u understand about exchanges. Forgive me, Father. For-
·e me and let Jesus live in my heart as King. I want only to
ve You now. I'm not worthy to be a son, but I will happily
a servant." Angeline's words brought immediate comfort.
·y didn't offer her an answer to her plight, but they did

give her the peace that God was now in control. And for
first time in her life, Angeline knew she'd truly come hon

Getting to her feet, Angeline picked up the Bible and
ished reading about the prodigal. He too pled his case to
father and his father, like her Heavenly Father, accepted h
home with open arms. "For this my son was dead, and
alive again; he was lost, and is found. And they began to
merry," Luke fifteen, twenty-four stated.

"I want to be merry, Lord," she whispered, "and I w
Gavin. I want us together and I want to share his life. Ple
help me to free him from his captivity and if I can't help h
then please, God, please don't let me harm him with my ca
lessness."

Angeline's first thought was that somehow, some way,
had to get to Gavin. But how? And even if she got th
how could she free him? No doubt Douglas would have
him guarded by his two friends. "What do I do?" she q
tioned aloud. Then as if her mother were standing beside
Angeline remembered her saying, "God guides our every s
Angeline, but we still have to be the one to pick up our
and move forward. When we do, we find out that He
there all along, just waiting for us to trust Him." Ange
smiled. She'd move forward and trust God to show her w
to do.

Feeling revived, she stripped out of the jacket and skirt
wore and went to the wardrobe. She wanted to find so
thing attractive, yet sedate. She needed to find Douglas
try to talk some sense into his head. She would plead
Gavin's life and she would happily offer up her own if ne
sary. Flipping through the dresses, Angeline gave each
careful consideration. She didn't want to encourage Dou
to believe her truly happy with their arrangement, yet

ted to keep his eye on her.

black satin gown crossed her eye and Angeline pulled it
n the wardrobe to consider it. It was absolutely stunning
i its flared skirt and fitted sleeves. The bodice was cut
, but then overlaid with a fine, black lace that came high
was secured to the neck with pearl encrusted, black vel-
ribbon. Angeline immediately knew it was the gown she
uld wear. Digging through the dresser drawer, Angeline
nd that Willa had thought of everything. Beautiful black
gloves were carefully resting beside white and rose col-
d ones, and beautiful things to wear underneath the dress
e waiting just one drawer down.

ngeline quickly went to work. She knew Douglas and
la were to have dinner together and what happened after-
d would be anyone's guess. She washed and dressed,
ng that the hour should still afford her enough time to
h them in the dining hall.

Vith rapid brush strokes, Angeline quickly twisted her hair
a stylish chignon and looked at her face in the mirror.
couldn't do much about her eyes. They were red, but
ed more like she'd missed many hours of sleep rather
spent many hours in tears.

t'll have to do," she said aloud and made her way to the
r.

utside, she was surprised to nearly run into a man who
trying to unlock the door adjacent to hers.

'm so sorry," she said and tried to back up.

he older man steadied her and smiled. "Angeline Mon-
My, my, but you've grown up to be a beautiful young
nan."

Dr. Jacobs!" Angeline exclaimed. The man was a good
nd of her father's. "How nice to run into you here. Are

you taking some time away from your practice?"

"No, I'm afraid it's all business for me. I'm here to atte
a lecture," he said with a smile. "What about you? You lo
like you're on your way to some place important."

"Oh, it's really nothing. I've been kept very busy helpi
with the suffrage cause, but I'm hoping to go home very soo

"You look quite tired," he stated in a concerned tone. "A
you all right?"

Suddenly a thought came to Angeline. "I am tired," s
admitted. "I haven't been able to get much rest." *It certai
wasn't a lie,* Angeline thought with relief. She wanted
rescue Gavin, but she didn't want to sin against God in or
to do so.

"You mustn't let it take its toll on you, Angeline." T
doctor's words led Angeline in exactly the direction s
wanted to go.

"I know," she said with a sigh. "Perhaps you could g
me something to help me sleep at night. Denver is suc
noisy city and this hotel has so very much going on. . . ." S
let her words trail off, hoping it was enough to elicit sym
thy from the old family friend.

"Of course," Dr. Jacobs replied. "I have some excell
medication for just that purpose." He reached into his
and pulled out a small vial. "A little of this in warm milk v
put you to sleep in no time. Just don't mix it with alcoho
you'll sleep a whole lot longer than you planned."

"You mean it would kill me?" Angeline asked, trying h
to sound horrified.

"No, no," the man answered. "Not unless you used
whole bottle. It's just that the effects are magnified with
cohol, but I don't imagine that's a concern for you anywa

"No, of course not," Angeline smiled. "Thank you so mu

, Jacobs. I will tell my father how very kind you were to
. I'm running a little short of cash, but if you would send
n a bill for this medication, I will personally see to it that
 paid."

'Nonsense. It's my pleasure to help. Now you run along
 d tell whomever you are meeting that you have doctor's
 ers to be in early tonight."

'I will," Angeline said with a smile. She hurried down the
 lway and felt for once that the answer to all of her prayers
 re held in her hand.

&

 ook almost a half an hour but by the time Angeline was
 ished, she was more than confident the plan would work.
 nding outside the room where Douglas had taken her and
 vin earlier, Angeline could only pray that they hadn't moved
 a. She also prayed that Douglas would be nowhere in sight,
 erwise she was certain her scheme would fail.

 Knocking lightly on the door, Angeline was relieved to find
 one Douglas had called, Joe answering the door.

'Whatda ya want?" He growled the question.

'I've brought you boys some refreshment," Angeline said
 d batted her lashes coyly. "Douglas thought you might
 oy some food."

 he man leered a smile, giving Angeline the once over and
 owed her into the room. "Look at this, Ralph. Baker must
 softenin' a bit. He let his woman bring up some eats."

 Good thing too," Ralph replied and did a double take when
 spotted Angeline. "Whew! I thought you were a looker,"
 said and sported a grin which revealed several missing
 th. No doubt acquired, Angeline presumed, from the fist
 ich had left his nose permanently listing to the left side of
 face.

"What'd ya bring?" Joe asked, taking the tray fr◦
Angeline.

Angeline refused to look at Gavin for fear she'd lose ▮
nerve. If she had seen his face, she would have found a stunr
look of anger and fear. Gavin couldn't believe she'd
allowed herself to come into such peril. He wanted to fo◦
her attention, but knowing Angel as he did, he knew it wo◦
only interfere in her plans. No, if Angel wanted to catch ▮
eye, she knew all she had to do was glance his way, Ga◦
reasoned. *I have to be quiet,* he thought, then glanced at ▮
again and swallowed hard. *Where in the world did she ▮
that dress?*

"I hope you like ham sandwiches." She rather purred ▮
words. "I also brought coffee."

"Ugh! That all?" Ralph asked, taking a look at the tra◦
contents when Joe put it down.

"Well, you know how it is, boys. Douglas figured you mi▮
like something to help flavor that coffee." Angeline produ◦
a quarter bottle of whiskey and poured a generous amo◦
into each cup of coffee. She smiled at both men then, hav◦
no idea how seductive the whole thing looked to Gavin.

The men eagerly took the treat and without so much
thank you, slammed it down and asked for the remaining c◦
tents of the bottle. Angeline shrugged her shoulders and sha◦
the whiskey between the two men. "Sorry there wasn't mo◦
but you know how it is these days. It was hard enough jus◦
get this much. I suppose you can get something else late◦

"That is if Baker turns us lose. You and him patch thi◦
up, eh?" Ralph asked her, helping himself to a sandwich.

Angeline nodded, still refusing to look at Gavin. She ▮
painfully aware that he was watching, but she knew ▮
couldn't see his expression just yet. It would be her undo◦

sure.

'Certainly. Douglas and I have an understanding and I've
·mised to be most cooperative. I never knew what a help-
man he could be." Angeline hoped she sounded convinc-

"Helpful, eh?" Ralph seemed unconcerned and yawned with
mouth full of sandwich. "Hey," he called to Joe. "Kinda
·rm in here isn't it?"

·oe suppressed his own yawn and nodded. "I'll open the
·dow," he said and put his empty mug on the table.

Angeline wondered silently how long it would take the
·eping medication, via the whiskey and coffee, to drug the
·n into sleep. They were already showing signs of fatigue.
·ase God, she prayed, *don't let it be much longer.*

Ralph sat down and yawned again. "I've been working too
·ny hours."

·oe finished opening the window and stuck his head out
·) the crisp night air. "Me too," he grumbled and pulled
·k inside.

Angeline felt her nerves begin to fray. "We could play
·ds," she said as though the men had complained of bore-
·n instead of exhaustion.

·oe shook his head and sunk into the nearest chair. "I don't
·k so." His eyes were drooping and his speech sounded
·htly slurred.

Angeline couldn't risk a look at Ralph without having some-
·ng to say. "How about another sandwich, Ralph?"

"Huh?" Ralph yawned and put his head down on the table.
·iink I'll just rest for a minute."

·ngeline held her breath and looked back at Joe. "I guess
·uglas really is working you too hard. I'll have to speak to
·i about it." She waited for a response from Joe, but his

thick eyelids were closed and a light snoring was already co▮
ing up in reply.

Ralph, too, began a kind of duet with Joe, snoring in lo▮
exhales, while Joe inhaled. Angeline refused to move a▮
refused to look at Gavin. She had to be certain Douglas' thu▮
were asleep.

Tiptoeing to Ralph, she shook him hard and only succeed
in breaking his rhythm of breathing for a moment. "Ralp
wake up," she said and shook him again. He was out cold

Moving to Joe, whose head bobbed up and down on l▮
thick chest, Angeline repeated the action. "Joe, wake up
Nothing! Not even a snort or a cough to indicate she'd ev▮
disturbed him.

All right, she thought. *That's done. They're both aslee▮
Now I get Gavin untied.* Straightening up, Angeline felt l▮
head grow light. With a pale face, she turned to look at Gav▮
just as her knees gave out and she sank to the floor.

seventeen

ngeline steadied herself against Joe's bulky leg. *I can't
int,* she thought and caught the look of concern in Gavin's
es. Poor Gavin. She smiled weakly at him, but neverthe-
ss it was a smile.

"I suppose you're wondering why I came here today," she
gan as though about to offer a lecture. Sucking in her breath
d using Joe for support, Angeline got to her feet and ad-
sted her skirts. Looking back at Gavin, she could see his
sed eyebrows.

"You like it?" she questioned, moving toward him in small
sitant steps. "It's another of Willa's dresses," she mused,
ing hard to keep her nerves steadied with the casual ban-
. Gavin nodded, wishing he could hurry her.

Angeline felt better after the first few steps and hurried
ward Gavin. She worked at the knotted scarf they'd used
gag him with. "Oh, Gavin!" she exclaimed, pulling at the
terial. "I'm so sorry I got you in all of this. I promise to
ke it up to you and I promise not to be any more trouble."
She pulled the material from his mouth and planted her lips
mly on his, much to Gavin's surprise. She pulled away,
ting his stunned expression. "I'll go anywhere with you
d do anything you tell me. I love you, Gavin!"

"You sure took your time coming to that conclusion, An-
," he finally said with a stern expression replacing the
ocked one. "I hope you're quicker about getting me out of
se ropes."

Angeline smiled and pulled up her skirt just enough to re veal a knife carefully tucked into her knee garter. "I am completely prepared to assist you, Mr. Lucas." She pulle the knife out and quickly sliced through the ropes.

Gavin came up off the chair like it was on fire and pulle Angeline into his arms, crushing her against him. For se eral moments he did nothing but hold her and for Angeline was enough. She clung to him, needing to feel strong agai It was all so right and she wondered silently how she cou have ever doubted that her place was with him.

"Did he hurt you, Angel?"

"No," she assured Gavin. "He didn't lay a hand on me. H did, however, tell Willa that we were to be married. They' planning a big, public wedding even now as we speak."

Gavin frowned and held her even tighter. "Over my dea body."

"It nearly was," Angeline replied flatly.

Voices sounding in the hallway disturbed their reunion a with the grace of cat, Gavin flew across the room and lock the door. With a finger to his lips, he pointed to the ope window.

Angeline paled and shook her head. She had an idea wh Gavin had planned and if her assumptions were correct, the was absolutely no way she was going to agree to the arrang ment.

Gavin crossed the room and took her in hand, with Angeli frantically shaking her head in protest. He pulled her clo and bent his lips to her ear. "I thought you said you'd follo me anywhere." He was grinning from ear to ear as he put h head out the window.

Angeline was terrified and shaking so hard she didn't thi she'd be able to move. The voices in the hall grew loud

...d one of them clearly became recognizable as Douglas. ...ithout second thoughts, she was out the window and stand-...g beside Gavin on the ledge.

Trembling with her back against the cold brick wall, ...ngeline thought she would die. She felt Gavin's warm hand ...n her arm and prayed God would rescue them from their ...rch. She heard Gavin lower the window and scoot closer ...her.

"It's going to be alright, Angel. You'll see."

"Oh, Gavin," she said and her voice was full of emotion. ...hat if I faint out here?"

"You won't," he said confidently. "Open your eyes and ...ok at me, Angel." She did without considering the conse-...ences. "God's with us. He's been with us from the start, ...t I think maybe you're just learning that. I love you and ...m not about to let anything happen to you. Especially not ...w that you've agreed to be my wife. You will be my wife, ...on't you, Angel?"

Angeline looked deep into Gavin's eyes. There was barely ...ough light from the window to reflect the love he held for ...r there. "If we live through this," she whispered, "I'll most ...atefully marry you."

Gavin chuckled and kissed her forehead. "Good, now don't ...ok down and keep quiet. Someday you can tell our children ...w I proposed on a ledge three stories above Denver." ...ngeline swallowed hard and nodded.

The words were no sooner out of Gavin's mouth when a ...orm came up from the hotel room inside. Angeline could ...ar Douglas raging and knew that he'd found his men sleep-...g and Gavin gone. She began trembling anew and felt Gavin ...ueeze her arm.

Oh God, please help me to be strong, Angeline prayed.

She shifted her weight and felt the satin skirt wrap around h—
legs. She had to be careful or she'd cause them both to fal
Gently, she eased her body back into its original position ar
felt the dress free itself again. Relieved, Angeline decide
that if she had to stop breathing in order to remain in on
position, she would. She couldn't jeopardize Gavin's li
again.

The voices from inside the room ceased and when the do—
slammed, Gavin braved a look into the room. Douglas ha
apparently gone in search of Gavin or Angeline, he surmise
Sliding the window up, Gavin pulled at Angel's arm. "Con
on," he said softly. "Just take little side steps. I've got
good hold on the window sill, you aren't going to fall."

Angeline forced her feet to move, but she felt like she w
going nowhere. "I can't do this, Gavin," she moaned, certa
that she'd be the death of them yet.

"Yes, you can, you're almost there," Gavin encourage
"Now, I'm going to step back and let you in first. Can ye
pull up your skirt so that it doesn't bind your legs?"

"Sure," Angeline said and reached for her skirt with h
free hand. "Are you sure this isn't just a ploy to get a look
my legs?" She tried very hard to sound teasing.

"Seen 'em already," Gavin answered in good humor, "wh—
you pulled the knife and on the way out here."

"Oh," Angeline replied nervously, but nevertheless smile
She lifted her leg to the window sill. "I can't say I get bor
with you, Mr. Lucas."

Gavin laughed and helped her through the window and in
the hotel room. Quickly following her, he pulled Angeli
into his arms and kissed her soundly. "I can't imagine li
without you, Angel."

"Nor I without you," she admitted. "I'm afraid it's n

stupid pride and stubborn determination that's nearly gotten you killed not once, but twice. Gavin, I would have died if I'd caused you to be hurt again."

"Shhh, don't talk like that. God knew what He was doing. I've never been out of His care and I know our mas have never stopped praying for us the whole time we've been gone."

"Yeah, and you know how they can nag," Angeline grinned. "Poor God must have had an earful by now."

"We should call and let them know we're coming home. Let's go to my room and get my stuff, then we'll go to your room and get yours." Gavin didn't wait for her reply, but quietly opened the door and looked down the hall. "It looks clear, come on."

Gavin led Angeline through the dimly lit hall. They passed without incident to Gavin's hotel room, where he unlocked the door and put his finger to his lip. Quietly pushing the door open, Gavin snapped on the light and surveyed the room. It was void of any uninvited guests, so he pulled Angeline into the room and slammed the door shut.

Angeline felt her heart in her throat. It was pounding at an insane rate that left her feeling breathless. "Are we safe here? Remember, Douglas knows your room number."

"He knows the room that Gavin Lucas is registered to. I wasn't stupid enough to underestimate him this time. This room is registered under my granddad's name."

"Oh?"

Gavin grinned. "Jason Intissar, at your service."

Angeline smiled and hesitantly noted the intimacy of the room. "We'd better get out of here. I'm afraid my reputation won't survive a visit to a man's hotel room."

"Now we have to get married, Angel," Gavin's lopsided grin only broadened.

"Guess so," she said, trying hard to sound disappointed. "You think you can tolerate life with a suffragette? I make a pretty good speech if I do say so myself."

"I know. I heard you in Santa Fe."

"I didn't know that!" Angeline exclaimed. Her eyes were shining with pleasure that he'd taken the time out to listen. "What did you think?"

"I think you could talk a guy into just about anything," he said softly and his eyes warmed with a sparkle of mischief. He took a step toward her. "At least I know you could talk me into just about anything."

Angeline's eyes widened. "I knew coming to your hotel room was just a trick. Wait till I tell my dad!"

"Ahh, I seem to remember that battle cry from your childhood. Good to see you got some of your spunk back," Gavin said and turned away to reach under the bed for his suitcase. "Let's go."

"Aren't you going to get your things?" she questioned.

"They're all in here." He shrugged his shoulders at her surprise. "I've learned to live on the run, what with following you all over the countryside."

Angeline shook her head. "It won't happen again, I can assure you."

"Ready to settle down, eh?"

"Very ready."

Gavin seemed more than a little pleased to hear the news. "Come on, let's go get your stuff."

Angeline stopped him, the look of grief marring her sweet face. "Please, let's just forget it. You know they'll be there. That's the first place they'll look. They won't have expected me to manage your rescue, so I'm sure Douglas came first thing to my room, thinking it would be the first place you'd go.

"It's all right, Angel. No one is going to stop us now."

"Please, Gavin, I can't bear it. I can't stand the thought of oing there for a few of my baubles and trinkets and have it ause your death." She clung to him, her eyes wide with fear. I'd gladly give my life for yours, Gavin. Stay here and I'll o, but don't come with me."

Gavin put down his case and encircled Angeline with both rms. He could feel her shaking as though she might never top. "God is in control. You do believe that, don't you?" Angeline nodded ever so slightly. Her hold on Gavin tight-ned, however.

"You belong to Him, don't you?"

"Yes," she whispered weakly. "I might not have until ear-er this evening, but I do now."

"God will protect us. Remember that verse in the Psalms, Angeline," he said, calling her by her full name. She looked p at him, shaking her head.

"Which one?"

"Ninety-one, verse eleven."

"I don't think I do," she said, struggling to remember.

"For he shall give his angels charge over thee, to keep thee all thy ways." Gavin lifted her chin to look deep into her iolet-colored eyes. "You're an angel God gave me," he whis-ered. "Just one of many. We're surrounded by them and ey have been given charge of us by God Almighty Himself. an you doubt that anything but the very best can happen ow?"

Angeline tried to let the words dispel her fear. "I want to elieve that. I truly do, but it seems foolish to test God by oing after material things that mean nothing to me."

"Do you trust Him, Angel?" Gavin questioned then added, Do you trust me?"

Angeline realized that never had she been so certain of any thing in all her life. God had given her new life. He'd helped her rescue Gavin. How could she believe He'd let her down now? "I trust you both," she stated clearly. "I'll do what ever you want."

"Good girl," he said and kissed her forehead. "Let's go get your things and go home."

Angeline held him back for just a moment. "Could we pray first, together?"

Gavin smiled a gentle, sweet smile at her. It gave her all the strength in the world and left her with no doubt that she was doing the right thing. "You bet."

eighteen

ngeline jumped at every sound, most of which seemed to
me from her. The black satin swished nosily, and despite
e carpeted floors, Angeline felt as though she was clump-
g instead of tiptoeing. The further they went, the worse it
as.

Angeline felt her chest constrict as she tried to keep from
sping for air. Her heart alone pounded so loud that she just
ew it would give them away. She followed Gavin closely,
raid that at any given moment, Douglas would jump out
ith a gun and shoot them both dead. Twice, Gavin had to
ll her along, but did so with a look of reassurance that made
ngeline feel better.

They hadn't gone all that far when Gavin spotted a bellhop
d called to him. "Wait here, Angel," Gavin said and slipped
vay to speak in a hushed whisper to the boy.

Angeline had no idea what Gavin was up to and further
ore she didn't believe she really cared. *I've had about as
uch adventure as a body can stand,* she told herself. It
as easy to think of going home and even easier to think of
ing it with Gavin at her side. Wringing her hands, Angeline
as relieved when the boy nodded enthusiastically and ac-
pted some coins from Gavin. Now if she could only talk
avin into forgetting this nonsense about her things.

When Gavin rejoined her, Angeline slipped her arm around
m coyly and batted her lashes. "We could just leave," she
ggested with a nod at the stairs leading down. "It'd get us

153

home just that much quicker."

Gavin laughed and shook his head. "No."

Angeline turned and put both arms around his neck. "I promise I won't ask for another thing."

"No, Angel." Gavin stopped laughing as she raised herse up on tiptoes and pressed her lips to his. "Angeline!"

"Oh, all right," she said and walked away in complete d jection. Grabbing handfuls of her skirt, she headed up t staircase. "I thought you said I could talk a man into an thing."

Gavin followed her, chuckling at her mutterings. "Just wa until I get you home, Angel. Then you can talk to me all yo want."

Angeline had to laugh in spite of herself, but she quick grew quiet as they reached the last step. Taking her hand his free one, Gavin led her down the hallway to her room There was no need for Angeline to retrieve her key; she cou tell by the light under the door that someone was already i side.

Reaching out, Angeline pushed the door open and foun Willa standing in the middle of the room.

"It's about time!" Willa exclaimed. "Douglas and I ha been frantic."

"I'll bet," Angeline said softly.

"Where is Baker?" Gavin questioned, putting his case b the door.

"Why, he's out looking for her, of course," Willa stat and came to where Angeline stood already unfastening t buttons of the black gown. "Who are you?"

"I have to change," Angeline said ignoring Willa's que tion and moving to the bedroom. "I'll pack my things, Gav and be right back."

"Pack your things?" Willa questioned after Angeline's re-
eating form. Getting no answer from her, Willa turned to
avin. "What is she talking about? Who are you?"

"I'm Gavin Lucas and I'm taking her home," he replied.
Ve're leaving tonight."

"You're going to find that kind of hard to do, Lucas." Dou-
as Baker stood in the open door, filling it ominously as
ough he offered himself as some kind of barrier.

"You gonna threaten to kill me again?" Gavin asked, turn-
g to face Douglas.

"I don't have to threaten. It won't take all that much to
complish the matter."

"Douglas, save it for later," Willa said irritably. "Angeline's
there and she'll be hard enough to handle without you threat-
ing him."

"She'll cooperate plenty if she thinks I'm going to hurt him.
e, she's quite gone over him and that offers me all of the
ntrol I need."

"Not quite, Douglas," Angeline said, coming through the
or, suitcase in hand. She had dressed in the shirtwaist and
ue serge skirt, the only things left which belonged to her.

Douglas sneered in contempt at Gavin. "You think he's
ing to stop me?"

Angeline shook her head. "It doesn't matter what you say
do, Douglas. I'm not going to marry you and I'm not go-
g to keep your secrets." She put down the case and turned
Willa. "He's using you Willa. He plans to destroy the
ffrage movement through you. I heard him talking and he
lieves giving women the vote is a big mistake. He thinks
e're too stupid or uncontrollable or some other such non-
nse. Either way, he plans to see you ruined and put away."

Willa turned to Douglas, her eyes narrowing suspiciously.

"Is that true? Is that your plan, Douglas?"

Baker laughed and left the open doorway. He moved firs toward Angeline, but found Gavin a formidable wall betwee him and the girl. Instead of pushing his luck just then, Dou glas shrugged and moved across the room to Willa.

"You're an idiot, Willa Neal. Suffrage is a nightmare tha must never be allowed to continue. I will personally put fort every effort possible to see it squelched." He looked as thoug he wanted to put an end to Willa then and there and for th first time ever, Angeline saw Willa back away.

"I must say you were a convincing actor," Willa said in fearful, yet determined voice. "Did you tell Angeline abou your plans? Did you tell her that you planned to marry her t get close to her political connections? Did you tell her tha even murder wasn't beneath you in order to get what yo wanted?"

"I didn't have to," Douglas said with smug satisfactio "She overheard my plans and I took her and Lucas captive. threatened them with each other. It was really quite simple

"It's true, Willa. That's when I learned about Dougla plans for you. He threatened to kill Gavin if I refused 1 marry him and even afterwards, he said he'd kill Gavin if revealed to you his plan to put an end to the suffrage mov ment."

Willa was enraged. "How dare you!" She moved towan Douglas, no longer afraid, but sufficiently incensed. She trie to slap Douglas, but he easily warded off her blows.

"Don't sound so persecuted, Willa. You were usir Angeline yourself." He smiled confidently at the way Willa face turned ashen. "You wanted Angeline for nothing mo than who she knew and whose support she could get you."

She could tell by the way Willa reacted that it was all tru

t hurt Angeline deeply to finally accept what everyone had lready told her to be true.

Her reaction was not missed by Douglas. "You know, Willa, ou very might have pulled it off," he said smugly, "except ou weren't expecting to deal with someone of my caliber. 've been operating one step ahead of you, all the way. Learning your routines. Mapping out your routes. Now is the time or me to step out and put you in your place."

"Just what do you have in mind?" Gavin asked dryly from vhere he gone to lean casually against the open door.

Douglas seemed unconcerned that his back was to Gavin. Ie didn't even bother to look away from Willa's worried xpression. "There's a nice asylum near Chicago. I have some ood friends there who will ask no questions. I thought the hange of scenery would do you good, old girl."

"You'll never get away with it!" Willa declared.

"And who will stop me?"

"I will," Willa declared. "I'll tell everyone what a fraud nd reprobate you are. I'll expose every single thing you have lanned." She was nearly yelling at this point. "You haven't een anything yet, Douglas Baker. I'll see you ruined."

Douglas laughed sinisterly, causing Angeline to pick up er case and back away toward the door.

"No one is going to ruin me," Douglas said so softly it was early a whisper. "No one will believe you, Willa. You have o one but this addle-brained girl to back you up and she'll e my wife, so I'll have no trouble out of her."

"I'll never marry you, Douglas!" Angeline exclaimed. Never!"

"We'll see about that." Douglas' eyes raked over Angeline efore turning back to Willa. "Like I said, no one is going to elieve your story."

"I don't know about that," the voice came from a stranger outside the door to Angeline's room. The well-dressed man walked into the room, still writing notes on a pad. He looked up long enough to introduce himself. "I'm a reporter with the *Post*. I've stood out there long enough to take down just about every word, Mr. Baker. I think the public will find this story fascinating."

Willa laughed aloud and Douglas glared at her hard. "This means nothing. I have friends at the *Post*."

"Had friends, Baker," the man said, still writing. "Had friends. No one is going to want to admit to being anything to you after my story runs."

Angeline glanced past the man to Gavin, who had obviously expected the man's entry. She loved him all the more for his insightfulness. Beaming a smile at him, Angeline knew he understood her unspoken praise.

"See there, Mr. Baker!" Willa declared, feeling quite vindicated.

"As for you, Miss Neal," the reporter continued, "I'm sure there will be more than enough interest in you to generate a thorough investigation into your activities."

"You just hate me because I'm a suffragist."

"No, ma'am, I don't hate you or the suffrage movement. I just want to see manipulative people like you put in their place."

Douglas made a move for the door, but quickly backed away when two uniformed policemen revealed themselves from the hallway. Angeline took that opportunity to retrieve her suitcase, which Gavin quickly took from her. Then looping her arm through his and nodding with a smile of contentment on her lips, Angeline let Gavin lead her to the door.

"By the way," the reporter called after her. "You're Miss

Angeline Monroe, are you not?"

Angeline paused and smiled. "That's right. At least for now."

The man jotted down the information and motioned. "Who's the guy with you?"

Angeline didn't even bat an eye. "He's just about to become my husband!" Her reply shocked Willa and infuriated Douglas, while the reporter just nodded with a grin and noted the broad smile of amusement on Gavin's face.

"I'd say the groom looks pretty happy about that prospect," the reporter said with a chuckle.

"You might say that," Gavin answered for her, then swept her into the hall. "Ready to go home, Angel?"

Angeline looked up at Gavin with eyes that declared their love for him. "Ready," she replied.

❧

That night, Angeline fell asleep to the gentle rocking of the train. She felt free and so completely at peace that she no longer questioned what she'd do with herself once they were home, or what cause she'd seek out. Gone were her little girl selfish ambitions and the desire to conquer the world. Gone were the searches for causes of great magnificence to occupy her time and energies with. All she really ever wanted was the man she slept contently against and the stillness that God had put in her heart.

Sighing in her sleep, Angeline missed the look of contentment on her husband-to-be's face. Gavin relished the feel of his arm around her and the way her blond head seemed to fit naturally against his shoulder. Thoughts of the decision he'd made so very long ago came back in pleasant memories. In his mind he could see Angeline as a twelve-year-old pulling a wagon filled with half-dead kittens. She'd found them tied in a sack and left to drown in the creek.

"What are you going to do with those mangy things?" Gavin had asked her in his sixteen-year-old bravado.

"I'm going to love them," Angeline had replied, her lavender eyes wide with surprise that he should even question such a thing.

"Looks like they'll need a lot of it," Gavin had laughed.

Angeline was undaunted. "That's all right," she'd replied confidently. "I have a lot of love to give."

It was then that Gavin knew she had his heart. Without even concerning himself that she was just a child, he knew that she was the woman he'd one day marry. Now, with Angeline having come to the same conclusion, Gavin Lucas was truly happy.

"You do have a lot of love to give, Angel," he whispered against her hair. "And I'm just glad to get a part of it."

nineteen

Angeline took herself into the garden, away from the well wishers and the revelry of her wedding. The sweet rich scent of roses and honeysuckle wafted on the warm afternoon air and the vivid colors were startling contrast to the white gowned woman.

Angeline had wanted to wear an older style wedding gown, but neither her mother or Gavin's had married in a traditional manner and so it was necessary to search for just the right gown. She had finally managed to locate the perfect creation hanging in a dressmaker's shop in Raton.

The dress was styled after gowns popular at the turn of the century. It was fashioned out of heavy slipper satin with intricate lace pinaforelike flounces at the shoulder and along the bodice. The basque waist was snug and showed off Angeline's tiny twenty-inch waist to perfection. After arguing with the dressmaker for over an hour, Angeline finally settled on a price and purchased the gown. Now, after having worn it, receiving scores of compliments and the warm glow of appreciation in her husband's eyes, Angeline felt the ridiculously high amount she'd paid had been worth it.

Laughter and music rose up as the festival-like atmosphere engulfed Piñon Canyon Ranch. Angeline was glad that Gavin chose his home for their wedding ceremony. It had been a beautiful affair, with all of their friends and family present. Even John and James had managed to fenagle time away from the army, although when they showed up in uniform, flying an army biplane, Angeline wondered just how legitimate their escape had been.

The aeroplane had caused more of a stir than the arrival of Joelle Dawson, but not much more. Angeline had to laugh, to herself of course, at the way her brothers and every other man on the ranch, fell all over themselves to see to Joelle's needs. She was a beautiful woman, Angeline had to admit, and for once she didn't feel at all threatened.

Joelle was Nicholas Dawson's little sister, making her Gavin's sister-in-law, and it was announced that she would be living for a while with Daughtry and Nicholas, who were once again expecting a child. Gavin had good-naturedly teased Angeline at the announcement of the impending arrival that they would have to work hard to catch up. Angeline had flushed scarlet, but in her heart it was exactly the thing she wanted. A family, a husband, a home. That was the only kind of cause Angeline perceived as lasting.

Looking across the garden, beyond the ranch valley to the mountains in the distance, Angeline felt a sensation of contentment wash over her that she couldn't begin to describe. The ineffable feeling bubbled up inside until Angeline didn't know whether to laugh or cry.

"God You have been so very good to me," she whispered. "Thank You for the bountiful blessings. Thank You for all that You've bestowed upon me. I know now how the prodigal must have felt when his father placed the fine robe upon his shoulder and killed the fatted calf. You've given me more than I deserve and I promise to strive hard to be worthy of it all."

❧

Gavin stood in the adobe archway and watched his wife with intense interest as she moved about the garden. She was the most beautiful woman he'd ever seen and she was all his. He stood there silently, afraid to go to her, afraid to break the spell that seemed to have woven itself over her. She was radiant and everything about her countenance spoke of her happiness and joy.

"Thank You, God," he whispered softly.

He studied her for a moment, seeing her lips move as though she was speaking to someone. With a sudden realization, Gavin discerned she was probably praying. It blessed him in a way he couldn't explain. It was gratifying to be a part of her life and to know that he'd have a long, long time to love her.

&

Angeline fell silent and closed her eyes for a moment. Drinking in the peace and pleasure of the moment, she didn't hear her husband come up from behind her. She didn't even sense him there until he put his arms around her and pulled her back against him.

"I couldn't find you. I thought maybe you'd run off again."

"Never!" Angeline declared and hugged his arms closer.

"What are you doing out here?" Gavin questioned softly.

"Just thanking God for everything." She turned, giving Gavin a beautiful smile that lit up her lavender eyes. "I'm so very grateful."

"Me too," he said and kissed her lightly on the lips. "I still can't believe you're really mine. I mean, I prayed about it long enough. God knows that I nagged Him often enough and now, it just seems unreal. Almost like a dream."

"Ummm," Angeline said snuggling against his chest, her head fitting perfecting under Gavin's chin. "Then I don't want to wake up."

"I love you, Angel. I think I have loved you forever."

Angeline giggled. "Since you first saw me as a tiny, squalling baby?"

"Well, maybe not quite forever," Gavin chuckled. "After all, I was barely in pants when you came along."

"I know," she whispered. "Your mother showed me the most precious picture of you holding me. She said, 'And now Angeline, he'll be holding you forever.' It made me cry, because I knew she was right. Some how, from that one little picture, that one small, seemingly insignificant moment in my life, our love was born and grew to be this."

Gavin kissed her head. "Brides are supposed to cry on their wedding days, but not grooms. Too many more stories like that and you'll have me sniffling. Come on, lets take a little walk, I want to show you something."

Angeline released her hold and let Gavin direct her down the path that led away from the main house. "I've been talking to my dad," Gavin began, "and I know you said you didn't care where we lived, so I took it upon myself to plan our home."

"What?"

Angeline's surprised tone caused Gavin to frown. "Is that a problem?"

"Not at all, I just presumed from what you said that we'd live here with your folks."

"We will, for a time," Gavin said. He kept walking past the out buildings and fruit trees which his mother had faithfully nurtured into maturity. "But eventually we'll have our own place. That is, if you want your own house."

Angeline laughed and tried to keep from tripping over her gown on the rocky path. "What woman doesn't?"

"Good, then you'll like my surprise," Gavin grinned down at her.

Angeline felt her heart skip a beat whenever he looked at her that way. She could only imagine the joy of waking up to see that smile every day.

Gavin slowed his steps to accommodate her more hesitant ones. "See, I figured that we'd live with my folks while we build our own place. We'll want to be close enough that it isn't a chore to come over, but far enough away for privacy."

Angeline grinned up at him. "So we can talk?"

Gavin laughed. "Something like that. Fight too," he added. "I don't figure the spunk has left you in place of that wedding gown. I know we'll have more than our share of misunderstandings and problems."

"I'm sure you're right," Angeline said with a serious nod. "You are after all a very stubborn man and you can be rather serious."

"And you are a flighty thing, running from one cause to the next and always thinking you have to be the center of attention."

Gavin's words made Angeline stop and eye him cautiously for a moment. "Are we about to have our first fight?"

"What do you mean, first fight?" Gavin asked with a twinkle in his eyes. "I've been having fights with you since you were six."

"Yes, I do seem to recall a rather nasty incident where you tore my red sash and pushed me in the creek," Angeline said rather sternly.

"And I don't suppose that you remember what you did to me first," Gavin replied, hands on hips.

"I believe it had something to do with your lunch pail," she said with a mischievous look.

"Something like you took it and threw it in the creek," he answered. "With my lunch in it, I might add."

Angeline giggled. "Yes and then you said I could just go in after it and pushed me over the bank."

"Yes, but I had a change of heart and tried to be gallant and rescue you."

"I remember. You grabbed my sash to pull me up and it ripped off in your hands and I went backside first into the water."

"But you got my lunch pail back," Gavin grinned.

"Yes, I did and a lecture when I got home and no desert for a week," Angeline said with a pouting look on her face.

"That's nothing," Gavin said with a serious expression replacing the grin. "I couldn't sit for a week."

Angeline laughed and threw her arms around her husband's neck. "You really have loved me forever, haven't you?"

"Pretty much so. I guess I was just hoping you'd get around to putting me on your list of causes."

"I'm done with causes," she said firmly. "Now show me what you plan for us."

Gavin took her hand in his and they walked a little further down the path. "You see that valley over there?"

Angeline looked out across the open ground to where a small stand of trees grew beside a well fed spring. "There?" she pointed and looked at Gavin.

"Yes." He sensed her satisfaction with the place. "I thought we'd put a house just beyond the trees. We'll have seclusion and privacy, yet be close enough for a helping hand if we need it."

"And you can still work the ranch with your father and not have to be that far from home. I could even fix you lunch every day and make up for the lunch pail incident." Angeline spoke with a pride and contentment in her voice that warmed Gavin's heart.

"You made up for the lunch pail long ago, Angel. Just promise me that you won't go running off again and I'll be the happiest man alive." He took her in his arms gently as if he were afraid of breaking her.

Angeline looked up at him. For a moment she just watched him and when clouds passed over the sun, shadowing the land, she shivered. "I want nothing more than to stay at your side." She looked away with an awful thought running through her mind.

"What is it, Angel?" Gavin reached out to draw her face back to his.

"There's so much that could separate us, Gavin. The war in Europe is getting worse. I heard John tell mother we'll probably go to war before much longer."

"That's a very real possibility, but we can't let it ruin our happiness."

"Oh, Gavin!" she exclaimed and embraced him tightly. "I don't want you to go away. I can't bear the idea of losing you. How could I go on without you?" The shadows from the clouds seemed to make her feel worse.

"Don't," he said simply. "Don't take away what we have now, by worrying about what we might not have tomorrow. We don't know what God has planned for us, Angel. But we do know that He has it figured out and He knows what's best. He's in control, just like He was the night we were on the ledge together. Just think of the stories we'll tell our children."

"Men never understand," Angeline said, surprising Gavin with her dismal outlook. "Mother told me men face war with pride and patriotism." She pushed away, stepping on her wedding dress. She would have fallen if Gavin hadn't caught her. The move forced her to look at his puzzled expression. Reaching up her hand, she touched his cheek. "I don't want you to be heroic. I'd rather have you be safe and sound, right here with me."

"I'd like nothing better," he said, looking at her as if seeing her and the responsibilities of taking a wife for the first time. "I've thought a great deal about the possibilities of having to serve my country in war." He looked beyond her to the valley. "But in all honesty, that was when I was single."

"Being married makes everything different," Angeline replied softly.

"Yes, it certainly does." He seemed to struggle with something inside himself, more than with her. A look of frustration crossed his face and he walked away from her, stopping after just a few paces.

Gavin's silence frightened Angeline and for a moment she hadn't any idea what to do. Then without any real thought, Angeline felt the need to be with him. To somehow let him know that she could stand beside him, whatever came their way.

She reached out to him and Gavin turned, surprising her with a hint of moisture in his eyes. "All I've ever wanted was to build a home here, marry you, and raise a family. I don't want to play soldier and I don't want to fight a war I know nothing about," he said honestly.

"You were right earlier," she whispered. "We needn't borrow trouble. God is in control, just as you said. From now on, Gavin, my only cause will be to serve God faithfully as His child and to love you faithfully as your wife. Whatever else comes, whatever the need, we'll face it together."

Gavin smiled. "No more causes, Angel?"

"Positive." Angeline was glad to see his mood lighten.

"You sure about that? You've been so caught up in causes

most all of your life, I'm not sure you could function properly without your hand in some problem, somewhere."

Angeline laughed. "You and God will be cause enough."

Gavin took her into his arms and lifted her chin. "I love you to pieces, Angel, but I'll believe that one when I see it." He silenced her reply with a kiss. Then, testing her reserve, Gavin pulled away and added, "I heard tell there was a committee getting together to raise money to build a bigger school in Bandelero."

"Not interested," Angeline replied with a wide grin.

"Then there was that talk about knitting mittens and socks for the soldiers in the trenches."

"I never could knit," Angeline said even more confidently.

Gavin glanced upward. "And I guess you wouldn't be interested in knowing that Elaine Cody is coming to Santa Fe to work with the local politicians on suffrage."

Angeline's eyes widened. "Elaine? Coming to New Mexico?" Gavin glanced down at her with an "I told you so" smile, causing Angeline to bite her tongue. "That's very nice, Gavin. Perhaps she'll call on us and we can show her the ranch."

"Uh huh," Gavin said with delight in his voice. "Maybe she'll tell you about the war orphans."

"What war orphans?" Angeline questioned almost sharply.

"The ones whose folks have died in the war. They're trying to raise money to. . . ."

"Gavin Lucas, you aren't being fair!"

"No, I'm not," he laughed and brought her back into his arms.

"I said no more causes and I meant it," Angeline restated, then a look of consideration passed over her expression. "Of course, I didn't know about the war orphans and Elaine was very nice to me in Denver. . . ."

Gavin kissed her before she could say another word. I
looked as if Angel's causes were about to strike again. "Jus
so long as I'm in there somewhere," he whispered against he
lips.

"Always," Angeline murmured with a smile. "Say, Gavin,'

"Huh?

"What do you suppose those war orphans need most?"

A Letter To Our Readers

ear Reader:

order that we might better contribute to your reading
joyment, we would appreciate your taking a few minutes to
spond to the following questions. When completed, please
turn to the following:

Rebecca Germany, Editor
Heartsong Presents
P.O. Box 719
Uhrichsville, Ohio 44683

Did you enjoy reading *Angel's Cause*?
❑ Very much. I would like to see more books
  by this author!
❑ Moderately
  I would have enjoyed it more if _____

_____

Are you a member of **Heartsong Presents**? ❑Yes ❑No
If no, where did you purchase this book? _____

_____

What influenced your decision to purchase this
book? (Check those that apply.)

❑ Cover   ❑ Back cover copy

❑ Title   ❑ Friends

❑ Publicity   ❑ Other_____

How would you rate, on a scale from 1 (poor) to 5
(superior), **Heartsong Presents'** new cover design? _____

5. On a scale from 1 (poor) to 10 (superior), please rate the following elements.

    __Heroine   __Plot

    __Hero   __Inspirational theme

    __Setting   __Secondary characters

6. What settings would you like to see covered in **Heartsong Presents** books?_____

_____

_____

7. What are some inspirational themes you would like to see treated in future books?_____

_____

_____

8. Would you be interested in reading other **Heartsong Presents** titles?   ❑ Yes   ❑ No

9. Please check your age range:
   ❑ Under 18   ❑ 18-24   ❑ 25-34
   ❑ 35-45   ❑ 46-55   ❑ Over 55

10. How many hours per week do you read? _____

Name _____

Occupation _____

Address _____

City_____ State_____ Zip _____

Tracie J. Peterson's

WESTERN ROMANCES

__*The Willing Heart*—Alexandra Stewart must choose between starvation and salvation. Faced with an impossible ultimatum, Zandy comes to discover the true reason why Riley Dawson was sent into her world. . .and the hidden treasure of a willing heart. HP63 $2.95

__*The Heart's Calling*—Where Pamela Charbonneau goes trouble follows. As she schemes to accompany her friend Zandy Dawson and her husband back to Colorado, Pamela's wildest dreams could not contain what lies ahead. But Pamela also could not imagine a friend as strong and dependable as rugged Jim Williams, or a faith in God that she will test to the limit. HP116 $2.95

__*Forever Yours*—At twenty-three, Daughtry Lucas knows she will end up an old maid unless she can escape her overprotective father. Answering a newspaper advertisement, Daughtry become Mrs. Nicholas Dawson in a marriage by proxy. Can this marriage between strangers succeed? HP127 $2.95

__*Angel's Cause*—Angeline Monroe can't resist a worthy cause. The only one who doesn't applaud her activism, though, is her lifelong friend, Gavin Lucas. Political rallies, power struggles, and even riots are just a few of the challenges Angel faces as she struggles to learn whom she can trust. HP140 $2.95

Hearts♥ng

HEARTSONG PRESENTS TITLES AVAILABLE NOW:

······Presents······

Great Inspirational Romance at a Great Price!

eartsong Presents books are inspirational romances in contempo-
ry and historical settings, designed to give you an enjoyable, spirit-
ting reading experience. You can choose from 140 wonderfully
ritten titles from some of today's best authors like Colleen L. Reece,
renda Bancroft, Janelle Jamison, and many others.

When ordering quantities less than twelve, above titles are $2.95 each.

SEND TO: Heartsong Presents Reader's Service
                P.O. Box 719, Uhrichsville, Ohio 44683

Please send me the items checked above. I am enclosing $_____.
please add $1.00 to cover postage per order. OH add 6.25% tax. NJ add
5%). Send check or money order, no cash or C.O.D.s, please.
        To place a credit card order, call 1-800-847-8270.

NAME _____

ADDRESS _____

CITY/STATE_____ ZIP _____

HPS SEPT.

Heartsong Presents
Love Stories Are Rated G!

That's for godly, gratifying, and of course, great! If you love a thrilling love story, but don't appreciate the sordidness of popular paperback romances, **Heartsong Presents** is for you. In fact, **Heartsong Presents** is the *only inspirational romance book club*, the only one featuring love stories where Christian faith is the primary ingredient in a marriage relationship.

Sign up today to receive your first set of four, never before published Christian romances. Send no money now; you will receive a bill with the first shipment. You may cancel at any time without obligation, and if you aren't completely satisfied with any selection, you may return the books for an immediate refund!

Imagine. . .four new romances every month—two historical, two contemporary—with men and women like you who long to meet the one God has chosen as the love of their lives. . .all for the low price of $9.97 postpaid.

To join, simply complete the coupon below and mail to the address provided. **Heartsong Presents** romances are rated G for another reason: They'll arrive *Godspeed!*